Copyright © Roy Lester Pond, 2020

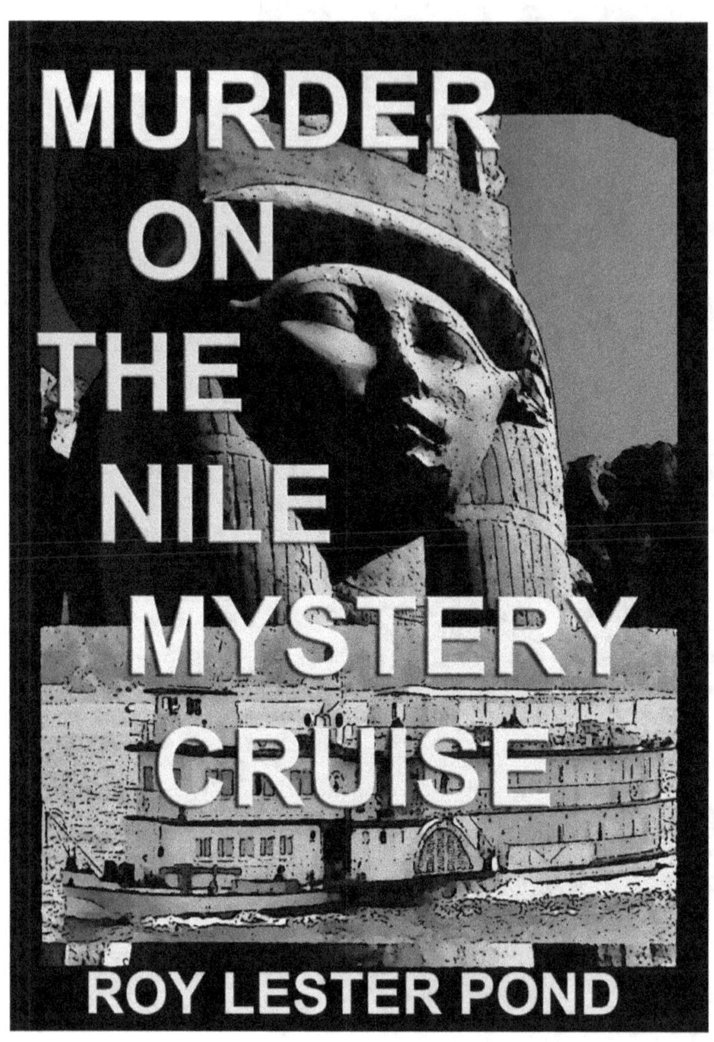

MURDER
ON
THE
NILE
MYSTERY
CRUISE
ROY LESTER POND

CONTENTS

A CAMCORDER VIDEO CAPTURES THE SETTING OF
THE STORY, AN ANTIQUE PADDLE WHEELER BOAT
ON THE MOVE - WHITE TIERS OF EDWARDIAN
CONFECTION, SIDE WHEELER PADDLES CHURNING
THE WATER.
S.S. 'BELLE EPOQUE': A LUXURY NILE STEAM VESSEL
FROM A GLORIOUS ERA.

VOICE OVER (Daniel Cane, cruise Egyptologist): "As
the paddle wheels of the *Belle Epoque* slowly turn like
the pages of a vintage Agatha Christie detective novel, a
contemporary 'mock murder' mystery game was
supposed to commence aboard the luxury Nile cruise
boat.
But all is not as it seems...

CHAPTER 1
Egypt, the ultimate movie set

"Egypt - a real life movie set... the ultimate setting for a mystery. You couldn't stage this stuff, could you?"
The rich old man waved his be-ringed hand at the panorama of the pyramids on view from his balcony at the Mena House Hotel.
He was Calder Hall, a vastly rich show-biz producer and sponsor of archaeology in Egypt and he had invited Daniel to his presidential suite for a mysterious meeting.
The pyramids looked as impressive as always, Daniel had to agree. But threatening too.
Jagged arrows of stone on the skyline, like mountainous warning symbols.
Hazard triangles.
Daniel sat across from two men at a coffee table. The second man was the rich man's attorney, Hyman Robbins.
The rich man, Calder Hall, was a shaven-headed octogenarian who put Daniel in mind of the craggy mummy of Pharaoh Seti in the museum. Daniel also noticed the old man's distinctive walking stick resting against the table, an antique Egyptian style stick with a golden jackal-dog's head that peered over the table. The dog's spiky ears were pressed back to smoothen the grip. Calder had suffered an early injury in a sports car accident and now walked with the aid of the mobility stick.
"I see you've still got Jack," Daniel said.
"Jack, my jackal-dog stick." He smiled. "You remember things, Daniel."

The walking stick had become a conversation piece when Daniel first met the rich champion of archaeology at a conference, about a year before.

"Isn't that Khentiamentiu, the early dog god of Abydos? Or maybe his other aspect, Wepwawet?" Daniel had said on that occasion.

"Very good," the old man had replied. "Most people just think Anubis, but of course Khentiamentiu and Wepwawet go back earlier as predecessors of Osiris the god of the dead."

"The Opener of Ways to the underworld," Daniel had said.

"That's it."

It had led to a discussion of a mutual interest in Abydos, Egypt's most ancient and holy burial ground, and a radical theory of Daniel's that the tomb of this canine-linked predecessor still remained to be found.

"I'll come to the point," the sponsor said now, turning his back on the view of the pyramids. "I want to hire your services as guest Egyptologist on a Nile cruise, but also as an investigator. The rewards will be greater than you could possibly earn in years of guest lecturing."

A few years away from the grind of guest lecturing, time to write more of those controversial books he longed to write and pursue those controversial theories he dreamed of pursuing, instead of playing ancient history tutor to fatuous groups of tourists in order to keep his 'body-and-ka' together as he termed it.

"Investigate?"

"Murder... mystery..."

"I'm an Egyptologist, Mr Hall," Daniel said. "Not a detective."

"I know. Call me Calder."

"Unless... this is one of those mock murder mystery games. Modern day Death on the Nile, in the spirit of Agatha Christie."

"See, he's deducing already. You are onto my game, Daniel. Very shrewd. And in the tradition of so many

mysteries, this one centres around a Last Will and
Testament. Mine. And a deplorable, gathered family.
Also mine, sadly. I am a dying man, you see. I have
weeks or so left to live." He sounded remarkably
fatalistic about it. This part might not be a game. Calder
had a skin pallor the shade of sun-bleached limestone.
"Are you going to be all right to go on a cruise?" Daniel
said. "Do you have an assistant to help you along?"
"A nurse, you mean? Pah! Can't bear mothering. No, I
only have Jack, my stick. And of course the boat's
registered doctor on board if I need any attention. But I
do have an assistant of sorts. A young protégé
filmmaker who is doing the story. I want this production
recorded, you see. To help me in this, I have hired
Mayet, a talented young Egyptian filmmaker who will
work unobtrusively with a camcorder, documenting our
little drama. I expect everyone to give her full support in
the project. She must have full all-access, at all times.
So here's how it plays. I give an opening warning to my
gathered clan that I'm reconsidering my Will, rewriting it
as I go, and making some drastic changes along the
way, depending on what I see in them. Hence my lawyer
Hyman is along for the ride. My family has been a great
disappointment to me over the years, Daniel. This cruise
will be my last scrutiny of them all. They'll be facing a
final judgement, just as I will be facing mine soon
enough. I've brought them all to Egypt on a special Nile
cruise for the occasion."
"That's a lot of trouble to go to."
"Trouble may be putting it mildly when it comes to the
possible repercussions when they hear my ruminations
on the Will and their prospects of inheritance."
"It's going to be controversial."
"And competitive. In such a family as mine it may even
turn out to be deadly."
"So a murder or two, then?"
"On the cards. And not just a whodunit, it may be a
who-is-going-to-do-it."

An intriguing family murder game.

Unlike Calder Hall, the lawyer sitting opposite him did not look like a game player. He was as formally dressed as an undertaker. Who else wore a waistcoat in Egypt? Daniel dubbed him Legal Suit.

"My client, Mr Hall is a quirky man, as he readily admits," Legal Suit said solemnly. "He likes putting people in situations."

"And I'm being put in one too?"

The old man now smiled.

"You are an Egyptologist and that's like detective work, digging for the facts. But you're also an informal man by your reputation, a man who will break with tradition."

"As well as being an entertainment producer of movies and television programmes, Mr Hall is very involved in Egyptology as a generous sponsor," the lawyer put in.

"Don't I know it," Daniel said. "He's every Egyptologist's dream."

"Egyptology is my useless passion in life," the shaven-skulled patriarch took over. "Though not as useless as my family."

"So what am I supposed to do on this cruise?" Daniel said.

"Act the guest Egyptologist," the old man said. "Bring ancient Egypt to life for them. Just because there's murder afoot, doesn't mean the cruise has to be murder all the way. It's never too late for my ignorant family to learn something about my favourite subject of ancient Egypt. You'll emerge as chief of the investigation later on."

"But why me? You could click your fingers and a dozen Egyptologists would jump on board."

"I like your fresh and controversial ideas on Egyptology. The academics with tenures and big archaeological missions in Egypt tend to get stuck in the weeds of Egyptology, qualifying everything they say to avoid criticism, clever people, but always peering over their shoulders to check on peer approval."

"They don't even talk to me. I'm not linked with any university mission in Egypt you see."

"They talk to me, and I never even attended university. Self made."

"But you have money to sponsor their archaeological digs."

"Ah, yes. And I'll be sponsoring your crime dig as you probe below the surface for clues. Let me show you the setting for our murder mystery cruise."

Calder opened a golden laptop on the table, clicked a few keys and swung it around.

An antique white paddleboat on the Nile splashed across the screen.

"The *Belle Epoque*. And that's the era the vessel came from, but now spankingly refurbished inside. A luxury side wheeler steamer on a voyage up the Nile from Cairo all the way to Aswan, on the world's longest river. This will be the setting for your investigation."

A fantasy setting for a mystery murder game.

It had its appeal. But Daniel wasn't a crime detective in real life. He was an independent Egyptologist.

"Me as a detective?"

"Yes, unusual casting, but intriguing. I call it casting against type. Real detectives are drab and boring, I know. I have a brother who was once a police detective. But you, being an Egyptologist, will bring an archaeological flavor to your ponderings. And a refreshingly different approach. You'll be on a dig beneath the hidden layers for answers. It'll all become clear when we gather on board before for our cruise. And of course you are welcome to bring your lady friend along. It's the full cruise. What they call the '*six hundred mile Nile*'."

"I'm sure Kate would find it irresistible. She loves games."

Maat and her feather of truth

CHAPTER 2
Feather of Truth

They threaded their way through the narrow, cobbled streets of *Khan el Khalili* Bazaar in Cairo, a sprawling, glowing Aladdin's Cave of tourist treasures.
Kate dived into a perfumery stall when a hawker stepped out and dangled a trinket before Daniel's eyes
"Genuine, Sir," said. He was an old man wearing a threadbare *galabea* and a grin.
Daniel immediately recognised the object in his fingers - an amulet of the goddess Maat in green faience. It depicted her neatly squatting, a long skirt stretched over her knees. A single ostrich feather protruded from her headband, her divine symbol. The 'feather of truth.'
Used in the underworld scales of justice to weigh the guilt or innocence of a dead person's heart and decide their worthiness to enter heaven.
"Not today, thanks," Daniel said.
Buying 'antiquities' from locals, even obvious fakes made for the tourist trade, was not something Egyptologists ought to do, even glorified tour guides like Daniel Cane.
He moved on a little further, eyeing a stall with exotic bottles in multi-coloured blown glass, like miniature minarets. They looked like perfume bottles, which made him wonder how Kate was going at the Egyptian perfumery stall.
He turned his head and found the old man still there, dangling the amulet.
"Special for you, Sir."
Daniel was about to shake his head again when he detected a certain appeal in the Egyptian's eye. Chronic

low tourism levels, exacerbated by a pandemic, had devastated the local population as much as low River Nile levels once did in ancient times.

The trinket was a pretty fake, he thought, taking it from him to look at.

Daniel eventually succumbed to the old man's grin and bought the Maat amulet.

Against professional instincts.

"What have you got?" Kate said, appearing with a small wrapped purchase in her hand.

"A little amulet keepsake," he said. "Maat, Goddess of truth and justice. See, she has the ostrich feather of truth on her head. Her priests used to paint a green feather on their tongues so that they would always speak and judge the truth, weighing innocence and guilt in fairness. And you, Kate? Did you find a perfume?"

"I bought this lovely fragrance for the cruise. Feathery and mysterious. Goes by the promising name of Fragrant Nefertiti. Do you like it?" She leaned forward, offering her cheek and ear.

Daniel breathed in the fragrance of Kate.

"You smell wonderful."

"And you're a big liar. Just a test. I actually haven't put any on. I bought it, untried on my skin, after one whiff of it."

Kate and her games. Tricking him again.

"You always smell wonderful," he said.

"But this perfume is new and I did wonder if you'd even notice when I put it on. Maybe you need that little amulet of truth..."

It was the first morning on the River Nile after leaving Cairo.

Daniel stuck out his tongue in the cabin's gilded vanity mirror.

The guest Egyptologist had slept in and was brushing his teeth in the cabin's marble and brass bathroom aboard S.S. *Belle Epoque,* when he'd spotted something odd.
But it wasn't the rudeness of his poked out tongue in the reflection that made him pull back as if offended.
It was a mark on his tongue. A blemish on the surface. He blinked blearily at his reflection. Coffee stain? No, not a stain, he decided, diving close to the mirror again. An image. *A green feather shape.* Painted on the surface of his tongue in outline.
A feather?
"Wha- tha- hell?" he said around his protruding tongue, like a victim of strangulation, his eyes splashes of wonderment.
He wiggled the tongue. The feather shape danced.
Some unknown Nile contagion? Maybe fur on his tongue from drinking old-fashioned gin slings with his girlfriend Kate the night before?
No, a distinct feather shape, drawn in what looked like green ink.
He spat out. He gargled with water. He brushed again. Rotating-oscillating bristles on the head of his electric toothbrush tickled the buds of his tongue, but failed to remove the blemish.

Then he recalled that in ancient Egypt the symbol of a
tall ostrich plume represented the goddess of Truth,
Balance and Justice, Maat. Priests of the Goddess of
Truth drew an image of her feather on their tongues
with green dye so that the words they spoke would be
the truth and now a dream of the night before came
back to him.

The Lady of Truth appeared to him in this dream,
blindingly beautiful as truth itself, a tall ostrich feather
stuck in her headband.

She spoke.

"Daniel, open your mouth."

It was a command that he had no difficulty in obeying.
He was already gaping in surprise at her transcendent
irruption into his life. Now she leaned forward with a
writing instrument in her fingers, a scribal pen in the
form of a pointed reed, which she scribbled over his
tongue.

Aargh.

The tickling produced the gag reflex; it was that true to
life.

But dreams were dreams and mythology was mythology.
This view in the mirror was real. A feather, the
hieroglyph for truth sat on his tongue. Unless he was
still dreaming, or mythology had broken into his life.

It triggered a memory of another incident, flashing into
his mind like light on the mirror from a porthole.

On the day before, he'd been approached by the hawker
in Cairo's *Khan el Kalili* bazaar and bought the Maat
amulet.

Now, a day later... this mystery in the bathroom vanity
mirror.

Maybe the mark on his tongue was a trick of his mind
and body, a mysterious appearance like *stigmata*, marks
of bloodied hands and feet that appeared on certain
devotees, matching the bodily wounds of Christ on the
cross. A phenomenon thought by some to be

psychosomatic in origin, though it was harder to explain
away in the case of newborn babies.
This mark had to be a trick.
But maybe he was blaming the wrong trickster.
That was it. It was not his brain or his body punking
him, he thought. It was his girlfriend Kate and her little
games.
After the gin slings the night before, he'd probably been
snoring with his mouth open, and Kate had playfully
sketched the symbol on his tongue using a green eye-
liner.
It was so Kate. She did that sort of thing. She'd once put
lipstick on him during an afternoon doze, because she
said he was asleep with a thoughtful pout on his lips.
Which was fine, except that he'd hurried off to an
engagement without checking his face beforehand.
And yet... Kate was a New Age adherent and for all her
game playing she held an earnest respect for ancient
Egyptian religion and its symbolism, more so than
Daniel did these days.
Levity from her about ancient Egyptian symbols and
mythology was surprising. Unless Kate thought he really
needed a lesson about honesty.
Should he accuse her?
Right then she appeared in the doorway of their marble
and brass bathroom.
"What about this sunhat on deck today?" she said,
sporting a wide brimmed black hat that made a pool of
her face.
"Honestly, the truth?" he said.
"What else?"
Daniel felt the feather image on his tongue meet the roof
of his mouth.
"It makes your eyes look like an anxious crab's peering
out from under a rock," he said.
"Too wide?"
A quick switch of hats to a grass one held in her other
hand.

"This one?"
How could he tell her? How could he resist?
"Thatched umbrella."
A frown now.
"O-k-a-y... "
She left the doorway, came back with a red hat. She tipped her head down to show him that this one had a narrower brim, making a red circle of her head as she bent.
"Traffic stopper," he said.
"You like it."
"No. Makes me think of a traffic light. The red light that drivers in Cairo regard as optional. I'm not a fan of hats."
"You've never said that before. What's wrong with you?"
He thought of accusing her, but the symbolism of the mark on his tongue struck him with the force of a revelation. It was as if he'd awoken with a mysterious gift from the dream world. He was afraid of talking it away.
Maybe I'll just hold my tongue for now, he thought.
He couldn't simply blurt out what had just happened. He needed to know more about his affliction.
What was this strange blight affecting him? He'd been helpless to resist the urgings of his tongue in his response to Kate.
Auto suggestion?
What had suddenly come over him?
Truth?
In a post-truth world?
A late onset of truthfulness in life might not sound like a huge problem for most people. But it could be awkward for him, he thought.
As a guest lecturer on a River Nile cruise, he was supposed to get along with passengers, not to mention his employer.

CHAPTER 3
A time of judgement

It was the first gathering on the river, the morning break, held in a sun-shafted Lounge that glowed on wooden panels and columns.

After coffees, teas and Egyptian pastries, as the *Belle Epoque's paddle wheels* softly tramped along the Nile, the family members arranged themselves on leather couches and plush chairs.

The patriarch faced them in a tall backed chair, like a pharaoh's throne, his jackal-dog walking stick held across his chest like a sceptre of Egypt. At his side, a royal court official, his lawyer, sat in an upright chair. Mayet, a young Egyptian filmmaker sporting an arty beret on her head, set herself up with her portable camcorder to capture the event.

Daniel swept a glance over the family. He had only a brushing acquaintance with detective stories and was not as comfortable about evaluating potential suspects as he was Egyptian artefacts, but he understood that the first thing an investigator should do was to examine the cast of players and notice any quirks.

They did not appear to his eye to be an especially deplorable family at first glance, except for the youngest son, a brooding young man in his thirties, prematurely balding in the old man's image. The young man sat rudely fiddling with a laptop on his knee.

A computer addict who didn't care that his open lid and tapping keys announced to the world that he was bored and did not want to be part of this game.

Then there was 'the sisterhood', two long-haired women
sitting close together, not twins, yet dressed in matching
colours. Both were knitting. They reminded him of the
twin goddesses Isis and Nephthys, who weaved the
wrappings for the mummy of Osiris. Their defensive
alliance clearly signaled: 'it's us against them.'
Next was the eldest son, Big Brother, his spreading legs
laying a claim to the space around him, his bulk
suggesting he would deserve the biggest share of
everything, including the inheritance pie, Daniel
thought.
Finally there was the family black sheep, Uncle Bryan, a
grizzled ex-cop, who according to Calder was discharged
for misconduct and repeated use of excessive force. He
looked a hard man with tight skin across his cheeks
and a controlled anger just beneath the surface.
The patriarch Calder Hall gave his family a probing
inspection through stern, hooded eyes, before speaking.
"Here we are. Like a scene from the judgment in the
Egyptian Book of the Dead. With Osiris presiding over
the weighing of the souls against the Feather of Truth.
And this *is* a time of judgement, because futures are in
the balance. Yours. I'm taking a last look at you all
before deciding about my Last Will and Testament. And
I don't have much time because the time of my own
judgment is approaching. I am hoping to recognize some
glint of redeeming virtue in you.
But first, my strict rules. After this morning's get-
together here, all personal phones and computers,
except mine, will be surrendered and locked in the office
safe of the Boat Manager until the end of the cruise. No
contact with the outside world is permitted. Nobody is to
leave until we reach the end, our terminus at Aswan on
the last day of November. We're all sealed in rather
splendid isolation, but then isolation is not so unusual
in this post-pandemic age, is it? The boat will stop along
the way at certain archaeological sites that interest me,

for short excursions, but otherwise our group will remain isolated from the world, come what may.
The captain, crew and staff are contracted to follow this rule strictly and stand to be rewarded for their observation of our agreement. This is almost certainly my last cruise and I am planning a linear progression all the way up the Nile to Nubian Egypt in the heart of Africa, like a return to the beginning of time. Our first stop of interest is Amarna and our guest cruise Egyptologist Mr Daniel Cane will now give us a little background flavor and colour and the benefit of his fresh eye on Egypt".

The family remained in the Lounge for the onboard lecture.
Not out of any newfound passion for the 'Splendour that was Egypt', Daniel surmised.
They sat under the watchful eye of the old man.
Calder's assistant protégé, the young Egyptian filmmaker took up a spot where she could record Daniel and the audience members.
"Some shocking truths about Egypt. I used to love ancient Egypt uncritically, like a new religious convert," Daniel said at a lectern set up by a pair of stewards in their purple livery, caftans and tasseled *tarbooshes* in the 1920s Ottoman mode. "I still love it," he told his audience who faced the lectern in the comfort of soft chairs and couches. They were forced to sit together but there was an animosity in the room like a hostile courtroom. "Today I see the truth. Our first stop and site visit on this Nile cruise will disappoint you - especially those who went to visit the pyramids and Sphinx of Giza before we embarked. Anybody?"
No hands went up.
"Unlike Giza, there's not much to see at Tell-el-Amarna. A few broken columns and foundations on a plain and some royal tombs in the distant hills. But it's a site of controversy bigger than the pyramids themselves.

Amarna, home of the heretic Akhenaten and his queen Nefertiti.

Here Akhenaten built his new city after abandoning the old gods of Egypt and the capital of Thebes for a brand new site of a city, which mushroomed in the desert like a nuclear test explosion. How did Akhenaten's whole new city come to be built on an empty plain in less than three years? Not a pretty story. You recognize these two?" Daniel pressed a button and an image came up on a screen of the distorted eighteenth dynasty king Akhenaten and his elegant wife Nefertiti.

Akhenaten and Nefertiti

"Swan-necked Nefertiti, in the world famous sculpture that resides in Berlin's *Neues* Museum. She has an unmistakable quality of classic loveliness. But then she is not the only serene-looking First Lady in history, ancient or recent, who has adorned the arm of a psychopath. Nefertiti has only one eye in this image, you'll notice.

For me, it's history's supreme irony. Why? Because I believe the beautiful lady of Amarna was one-eyed, metaphorically speaking. She turned a blind eye on the horrors of what was going on at her new city.

Today it's fashionable for Egyptologists to claim that the

pyramid builders were willing workers, perhaps the profession's agnostic reaction against the biblical whip and taskmaster scenes of epic movies. Yet the most casual glance at Egypt's monumental architecture tells us that ancient Egypt was no picnic for workers - whether they were prisoners, or Egyptians forced into state labour under the draconian *corvee* conscription system. Running away was a capital crime. Shirk and you could have your nose and ears cut off.

Workers may not have been 'slaves' in name and they may have been fed by the state and had their injuries patched up by medicos, but coercion was at the core of Egyptian monumentality as new research reveals.

More shocking truth. There is evidence that Akhenaten used forced child labour, children uprooted from their families in Thebes hundreds of kilometres away and brought to build his city with little hope of returning. What proof? Burials of children and teenagers in disproportionate numbers in Amarna. More than ninety percent of the skeletons have an estimated age as low as seven, with the majority of these estimated to be younger than fifteen."

Was his audience horrified?

Not much.

Certainly not Computer Man, who still went on secretly fiddling with his laptop at the risk of his father's disapproval and at a risk to his chances of inheritance. Maybe he needed a last, urgent fix before they seized his drug of choice and locked it away for the rest of the cruise.

Daniel continued:

"Children provided a handy disposable workforce for the pharaoh's fanatical ambitions, yet despite their tender age at death, these skeletons were riddled with traumatic bone injuries and arthritis from heavy load bearing. It's no co-incidence that Akhenaten introduced new smaller stone blocks for building. Junior-size *Leggo* blocks known as *talatat*, to speed up the process.

Instead of the cyclopean slabs used by his predecessors, these stones weighed seventy kilograms. Yet imagine hefting blocks of one hundred and fifty pounds all day long in the searing heat of Egypt's sun. Picture hordes of ill-nourished kids trying to manhandle them into place. Amarna may be a source of fascination to Egyptologists as the flowering place of a religious revolution and of a new artistic canon, but underneath, where the bodies lay, it was no Camelot, if you want the truth. Nor was Nefertiti as serene as she looked.

Nefertiti clubbing a victim to death in a smiting execution scene

Here's a scene from Boston Museum of Fine Arts that might surprise you." He flashed up an image of Nefertiti wearing her unique high crown.
"She still looks serene, but here she's holding a club in her hand and she's about to club a victim to death in a ritual execution scene.
The pharaohs were rather addicted to clubbing their enemies to death - in so-called smiting scenes of execution. Cracking skulls is probably the most persistently occurring image of pharaonic culture, but it's rare to see a queen poised in this menacing attitude..."
Daniel wrapped up his onboard lecture by concluding: "Incidentally, as a foreign Egyptologist in Egypt I am only permitted to provide lectures on board. By Egyptian law, licensed Egyptian tour guides must conduct group tours on sites. It's even frowned upon for a professional outsider to point at a ruin. Freelance Egyptian guides will be on the ground to help you. Any questions about Amarna?"
None from the family, but a comment from the patriarch.
"A refreshingly honest take on Amarna, Daniel," he said. "It's normally hallowed ground for Egyptologists."
Afterwards, as the passengers filed out, Daniel's girlfriend Kate was less then enthusiastic.
"How could you be so damning about Amarna and Ahhenaten?" she said.
"You mean how can I be an iconoclast about an iconoclast?"
"You're being odd."
"Maybe I'm finding a new streak of honesty. Do you suppose the truth about child labour in Amarna shocked our audience?"

"Worryingly, no. I heard some muttering that it was better than having youth violence and crimes on the streets."

"Law-and-order zealots. I wonder if they are going to be as caring about law and order in their own actions."

But of course this was only a game and they were playing the role of deplorables, he thought.

Quite convincingly though.

'Better lift my own game, he decided. 'Keep it real.'

Wasn't that the secret to successful acting?

"Let's get some air on deck," Kate said. "What do you say we go up and grab a sun-lounger?"

"You start burning without me. I'm going to stretch my legs."

The Egyptian Boat Manager, Mr Amira, advanced towards Daniel along the teak wood promenade deck, calling out a cheery "Good day, Sir," as Daniel approached him, adding: "Is everybody quite happy?"

"Convincingly, *no*, thank you" Daniel said. "But nobody could complain about your impeccable boat and service."

"Thank you, Sir," the round man said, smoothing away a flicker of puzzlement. "Do you happen to have your personal phone with you, Sir? We are collecting them."

'So the rules are going to apply to me, too,' Daniel thought.

"Yes, of course." He fished out an iPhone from a pocket of his cargo pants and handed it over with the twinge of unease he usually felt when parting with his passport to officials in Egypt.

"Any computers in your cabin, Sir?"

"None. I should be writing, I know, but no."

The Boat Manager placed the phone in a bag and moved on like a church usher going around with the offering basket.

"Thank you, Sir. Your phone will remain secure in my office, I assure you."

There weren't many passengers around. Maybe they'd gone to their cabins to collect their personal phones and computers before the round up.

Daniel approached the churning turmoil of a paddle wheel.

He paused on the deck above the side-wheeler housing, felt the bite of the paddles in the water under his feet.

Dig, dig, dig...

That's exactly what he must do as both an archaeologist and a detective.

Start digging. Try to anticipate trouble before it happened.

The watery march of the rotating paddles in the blue-green Nile and the steady spray gave Daniel a reassuring sense of momentum, a hope that he was getting the feel of the situation.

But was it an illusion?

Questions churned in his mind.

Was everything as it seemed?

Was he being drawn into a cleverly staged game? Or dramatic reality?

Maybe both.

The rich producer may have hit on the idea of combining a mock drama with a real life one?

To what end?

To punish his feckless progeny and at the same time have the satisfaction of mounting one last ultimate production before he went out in a blaze of glory?

The old man had hired the young filmmaker to capture the event, after all.

The symbol of truth on Daniel's tongue touched the roof of his mouth.

True or false?

Egyptologists were expected to be skilled at discriminating between fakeries and the real thing. Like the swift judgement he'd made of the Maat amulet purchased from a street seller at *Khan el Kalili* bazaar.

He'd dismissed it as a clever fake, but now he was beginning to wonder.
Was the family drama, taking place on the boat, fake or reality?
Reality?
Possibly reality television?
There was a startling thought.
Calder Hall was a big movie and television producer and it was not beyond the bounds of possibility that this whole affair was in fact a reality television show secretly being filmed and recorded under the cover of the girl's documentary.
Daniel inspected the deck and walls, seeking holes where hidden cameras and microphones might lurk, recording every step and word.
Was he under surveillance right now?
'I'm sure I don't look the part of a crime investigator,' he thought.
A casually dressed archaeology type in loose multi-pocketed clothing, with a field man's slouch, instead of the incisive figure of a Sherlock Holmes.
Yet big things were expected of him.
Clearly Calder Hall hoped that a trained archaeologist and Egyptologist might approach the challenge of a murder investigation in an entertainingly different manner. If Daniel failed, he might not only fail his employer, but also destroy any belief a television audience might have in the deductive abilities of Egyptologists.
'Ironic if I am the one carrying the flag for my profession', Daniel thought.
Stop it. You're being paranoid.
This is what it is.
A murder mystery game with an atmospheric cruise thrown in. That's the truth of it.
Forget play-acting detective.
What would an archaeologist do?

First, he would pace out and survey the site and its topography.
Boots on the ground archaeology.
Daniel paced the seventy-two metre long vessel.
Broad passages linked lavish grand suites at either end and eighteen luxurious cabins in between, all air-conditioned and spread out over two decks, with a shaded sun deck up top.
Glints of gilding, brass, stained glass and shining, curved hardwood met the eye everywhere, as well as antique hanging photographs of early Egyptian royalty, along with European gentlemen archaeologists and their ladies under parasols. He passed through observation saloons, bars, the 1930s style lounge and a grand candelabra-drooped dining saloon below. He also noted a compact, book-lined library.
The *Belle Epoque* was a far cry from the mean streets of detective fiction, he thought.

A murder mystery game with an atmospheric cruise thrown in

CHAPTER 4

A smiting

After his tour, he went up to the sun deck to find Kate, who lay stretched out on a cushioned steamer chair, still reading her book on Egyptian mythology.

He watched the riverbank sliding by, palm bursts of trees among emerald green agricultural fields, with mountains replacing the outlines of pyramids in the distance.

"Were you relieved of your phone too?" she said, looking up.

"Yes."

"I can't even take photos now. I feel naked without it."

She was doing a pretty good job already in her handsome turquoise one-piece bathing suit, he thought admiringly.

He dropped into a deck chair beside her.

In spite of Calder Hall's faith in Daniel's investigative abilities, Kate's shrewd eye and instincts might be a valuable addition to his armoury. "What do you make of the players?" he said.

"I suppose our host's family is going along with this murder mystery idea to humour the old man."

"They're not doing it with much grace."

"And it's probably no fabrication that Calder Hall has a Will in real life and they hope to be part of it in the end."

"Yes, that's where the game thing blurs," he said.

"It's early,' she said, 'and depends on what parts in the drama have been assigned to them. But at face value, it's obvious to me that the family hates the old man as much as he hates them. In real life, I mean, not just in some made-up scenario. Nobody seems to be acting here."

Perceptive Kate.

He'd picked up mutual feelings of rancour too.
"You mean they're truly that horrible? Then they probably deserve each other."
"Karma," she said.
"Or Maat at work," he said.
"Maat! Yes, I've just been reading more about your Maat. The ancient Egyptian goddess of truth, balance and justice. There are similarities with Karma. The good and bad you do in your life comes to haunt you in your life to come."
Was it the good or the bad he had done that had brought these intimations of Maat into his life?
He sat back, tried to relax.
After the heaving clamour of Cairo's population and traffic, it was good to be on the timeless Nile again.
Kate waved her book on mythology.
"Who is your favourite Egyptian god or goddess?" she said.
"I'm intrigued by Khentiamentiu of ancient Abydos, who is symbolised by a jackal-dog."
"I'll pick Maat," she said, startling him. "The beautiful lady of truth. Maat's Egyptian priests were the judges of Egypt, I've learnt. They wore a golden emblem of Maat around their necks."
Yes, and they also bore Maat's emblem in another place, he thought, though it didn't appear in many books on mythology.
Ironic, he thought, that I have been put in the role of judging the guilty and the innocent in a murder mystery game. 'Maybe I should wear the Maat amulet I bought. Around my neck on a string.'
He pressed his tongue to the roof of his mouth. No, he didn't need a Maat necklace. He had her mark on his tongue already, the feather hieroglyph of truth.
"It says in here that Maat had Forty Two Laws that were the forerunners of the Ten Commandments," she said. "When the dead came to be judged in her weighing scales in the Hall of Maat, their hearts had to be lighter

than a feather... free of all forty two sins."

"Some of those laws are almost identical to Old Testament ones," he said.

"Let's play a game," she said. "Imagine I'm Maat and you have to pass the test of my scales of judgement in order to survive in the afterlife." She flipped through to a page in her book. "Here. Answer me truthfully. Have you ever cursed anyone in thought, word or deeds?"

"Maybe a few hidebound Egyptologists."

"Have you ever stolen?"

"You mean used something in one of my books without proper attribution? Possibly, yes. I get tired of footnotes."

"Have you ever committed adultery?"

"I don't qualify. I'm single."

"No you're not."

"I mean unmarried."

"Y-e-s. But would you?"

"Get married?

"Commit adultery if you were?"

"That's not on Maat's list. And no, I wouldn't commit that sin, even if she was as attractive as you are in that bathing costume."

"Seduced another man's wife?"

"Never."

"Falsely accused anyone?"

"I hope not. In fact I hope I don't start. I'm expected to get things right in this investigation game."

"Have you ever been an eavesdropper?"

"No, but I'm not above it."

"Exaggerated your words when speaking?"

"Possibly in some of my archaeological theories, yes."

"I don't suppose you've ever stolen the god's offerings?"

"Probably, yes. When I was a youthful volunteer on digs, no doubt. Archaeologists take ancient tomb offerings and put them in museums. How am I doing?"

"You may pass. Enter the heavenly Fields of *Aaru*, Justified One!"

"Thank you. "

"Don't you just love the goddess Maat?" she said.

"Yes, but I could be cynical and say Maat was an ideology that kept the pharaohs in power for so long. Maat stood for divine law and order. Don't rock the boat and risk overthrowing the old order. Keep the balance of status quo. But the laws of Maat applied to kings too. They were charged with the responsibility of preserving Maat, or universal order. Maat was the most important divinity in Egypt. She was the glue in their civilization and deeply revered. The greatest offering any pharaoh could make to the gods was to present them with an offering of Maat's image in miniature."

"Like the miniature amulet you bought the other day at *Khan el Kalili*?" she said.

He nodded.

"But in pure gold."

"May I see her again?"

'I don't have her on me,' he wanted to say, but he couldn't raise the lie to his tongue. He dug the green faience amulet out of a pocket and handed it over.

She admired the little figure in her palm.

"She's charming. Will you part with her? Look, she has a little loop here that I can slip onto a string necklace. The goddess Maat doesn't deserve to be hidden in the tomb of your pocket, Daniel. At least, if I'm wearing her, you will get to see her."

'And she will get to see me, watch me.'

Why was that faintly disturbing?

'Don't be superstitious,' he told himself.

"Keep her."

"Thank you. I'll wear Maat for you on the rest of the cruise."

The Egyptian filmmaker Mayet made an appearance on deck, camcorder in hand.

He'd first met Calder Hall's young protégé at the embarkation and he was attracted to her breezy Egyptian friendliness and humour. The girl had used her camcorder to capture the arrival of each of the passengers on board the *Belle Epoque*.

"This is a bit like the arrival scenes in the old Love Boat television series," she had joked to him at the time.

"Maybe 'Murder Boat'," he'd said...

"Hello Daniel, Kate. Am I interrupting you two? Sorry." She didn't wait for an answer. "Daniel, I'd like to do a piece with you talking to camera, recording your feelings about the set-up of our Nile show."

"You go ahead," Kate said to him. "I'm going back to the cabin to find a necklace string."

"Where shall we do it?" he said to the girl. "Do you want me looking like a detective or an Egyptologist?"

"Oh, Egyptologist is fine."

"Pity we don't have a background of ancient ruins and archaeological treasures," he said.

"I suppose that's where Egyptologists spend most of their time."

"No, in a library actually. And there's one on board."

"Perfect."

The library, lit by a picture window had a desk and a collection of books on shelves. While she looked around for the best set up, he remarked:

"Your name, Mayet. That's Egyptian."

"Yes, I am Egyptian, although I lived with my mother in America for a time."

"No, I mean ancient Egyptian," he said. "It's another spelling of the name Maat."

"You sound amazed."

Disturbed by the synchronicity of it, he thought.

First the amulet thing, then the mark of the tongue and a now a female namesake of Maat right here on board with him. Fantasy, mythology and reality were not merely bumping, they were dissolving into each other.

"I am a truth seeker, I suppose," she said. "I'm a filmmaker. So the name fits me."

She chose side lighting from the window and sat him in a chair near the desk, with rows of books behind him, popular Egypt titles, with their covers turned outwards: *The Egyptian Book of the Dead, Historical Atlas of Ancient Egypt. Egypt from the Air. Dictionary of Egyptian Civilization, Ancient Egyptian Magic...*

"Okay, please be honest and as frank as you can, Daniel," she directed him. "I want to capture the human aspect of this voyage. I want you, as an archaeologist, pondering, as if you've dug up a puzzle."

Be honest?

He had little choice.

THE CAMCORDER LENS FOCUSES ON THE RUGGED, BUT THOUGHTFULLY POUTING FACE OF DANIEL CANE, EGYPTOLOGIST.

HE BEGINS TO SPEAK IN A CONVERSATION WAY TO THE CAMERA.

HE HAS FRONTED DOCUMENTARIES BEFORE AND KNOWS TO MAKE A 100 PERCENT DELIVERY TO CAMERA FEEL INTIMATE AND CONVERSATIONAL.

"Truthfully, I am all at sea here.

Yes, even though this is the Nile and we're cruising the world's longest river.

I don't normally interrogate people, only facts and artefacts. I prefer the solitude of ruins, deserts, temples and tombs... and deserted libraries.

I seem to feel eyes on me all the time on this cruise. Maybe it's this camera.

A confession. The tragic pandemic worldwide lockdowns we look back on actually suited my temperament. Social distancing was something I habitually practiced, like most writers and theorists. Enforced Isolation for me was as if the rest of the world had suddenly caught up. Or slowed down, to

match my life. But there's no social escape on a cruise boat of this size, even though it's half empty. Crew members outnumber the passengers.
A mock murder cruise in the Agatha Christie tradition was not something I would have put my hand up for, but it's all about mystery and mystery is what drives my interest in ancient Egypt.
It's said that archaeologists and detectives are kindred spirits. The only difference being that, for an archaeologist, the parties of interest, as well as the witnesses, are all dead. Mind you, a few of the parties of interest could soon end up the same way if this should follow the pattern of an Agatha Christie plot.
What do I think of the line up?
"Tolstoy wrote: '*all happy families are alike; each unhappy family is unhappy in its own way*'. I think a more truthful pronouncement on families might be: '*all families are ugly in their own way*'. But are they murderous?" He shrugged.
"A bit, I suppose. Think of Thanksgivings and Christmases. Don't most families locked up together feel a bit like murdering each other after a while? And the family on this cruise has been given a massive motive."

That night the itinerary called for a thirties-style dress-up at dinner.
A little jollity for a disgruntled family?
The boat manager provided a choice of costumes from an empty cabin turned into a dressing room, stocked with vintage costumes on hangars. Dresses, suits, feather boas, stoles, hats, coats, costume jewellery...
"A game within a game!" Kate said, her brown eyes shining. "Ooh, what fun! You've got to be a real detective tonight, Daniel. Poirot style. There's a grey three-piece lounge suit here and look, here's a black homburg hat."

"I hate hats."

"As you informed me. Now I'm getting my revenge. You have to throw yourself into playing a role."

"I thought I was playing a role."

"You've got to look the part. I fancy this green vintage frock to match my Maat amulet and maybe some sort of feathery hat or fascinator to go with it."

Feathers again.

The family played along, but that didn't mean they were going to play happy.

Dress-up had been mandated, so the family made a few concession to the occasion - a pith-helmet glumly worn on young Computer Man's head, headbands and sparkly evening outfits on the two sisters, a stuck-on Edwardian moustache drooping down the jowls of Big Brother. Uncle Bryan came dressed as a flashy thirties crime boss in a fedora, a black shirt and white tie and wearing big diamond cufflinks.

Calder arrived as a Lord Carnarvon type, echoing his role as a great patron of Egyptology. Legal Suit's concession to the informality of the evening was oiled back hair and a monocle.

"You look stunningly elegant, Kate, and that Fragrant Nefertiti fragrance is a hit."

"I didn't put any on."

"Yes, you did. Don't try to trick me again."

"Okay, I am wearing it tonight. Glad you like it."

Tonight? Was that a hint she'd worn it before? Or a playful tease?

Mayet, the young Egyptian filmmaker, stole the evening. She arrived in a pure white sheath dress, broad collar turquoise necklace and a headband surmounted by a tall white ostrich plume. Her light-caramel skin, dramatic eye-shadow and liquid dark eyes gave her a

look that was both vintage thirties and ancient Egyptian
in style, that peculiar convergence of the art-deco age.
Mayet had turned into Maat!
Startlingly so. Daniel's heart gave a kick.
The one jarring note was the camcorder bag
 I am being haunted by Maat, he thought.
Kate invited her to join their table.
"You are my favourite goddess," she said.
"And yet it is you, Kate, who wears the Maat necklace,"
the Egyptian girl laughed. "You look beautiful. And
Daniel, look at you! You are the picture of the detective
in the old Agatha Christie movies! Good evening,
Hercule!"
"'Ercule, please."
"You should wear that suit when I film you."
"Not a moment longer than tonight."
"I will join you for dinner, thank you, but first I must
take footage of the party..."
Mayet went off among the tables, stopping at each one
to capture the moment and record individual comments
of guests.
He tried not to stare.
Kate fingered the amulet on her necklace.
When Mayet returned to their table, she directed her
camera on them.
"What a pair. The great detective and a lovely socialite.
What do you make of the evening, Daniel?"
"It reminds me of tales of mythology and a story that
begins: '*And all the dead who had died that day were
gathered together on the Boat of Ra for their journey into
the underworld...*' Fortunately, though, our murder
mystery cruise has not produced any victims yet."
"And what do *you* make of this happy family gathering,
Mayet?" Daniel said as she tucked her camcorder into
its bag. "As an objective, outside eye on a curious
family."
"Not a happy one to be part of I would think. And none
of them very happy to be here. Except for Calder. But

tonight I can forget them all for a moment and enjoy dinner with two favourite people."

"What's it like working for him?"

"Calder? As a young filmmaker, I feel under pressure from him. He watches updates of my footage at the end of each day. He seems to like my work, but I feel I am being judged of course."

"As am I. I'm sure you don't disappoint him. But I can't say the same for me, being cast as a detective."

"Casting against type. Calder likes doing that."

An eternity cruising the Nile

CHAPTER 5
The timeless Nile

Travel itineraries ought to be printed in blurred type, Daniel thought. They established a rhythm that ensured the days would blur together, the more pleasant, the more out of focus.

And the time on the river was surprisingly hazy and dreamlike.

For Daniel, each day of the cruise aboard the steam paddle wheeler *Belle Epoque* was like threading dazzling gemstones on an ancient Egyptian necklace, turquoise blue skies reflected in a blue-green Nile - shining days, glittering nights.

A circle of breakfasts, teas, lectures, lunches, sunset cocktails and opulent silver-service dinners in the dining saloon. Dinners were a feast, but not the spreading buffet feasts of yesterday, Daniel noticed. In the new mood of social distancing, spreading dishes and jostling buffet queues had lost their appeal. The tradition Egyptian favourites were all still there however, grilled Nile perch, fragrantly spiced lamb kebabs, falafel, hummus and eggplant dips.

And afterwards, nights spent between fine Egyptian linen in an antique brass bed.

Daniel began to relax as their paddle wheels ploughed the meandering upper reaches of the Nile.

The old man sought out Daniel as he stood leaning on the rail, viewing the pleasantly static diorama of Egypt that looked as it had looked for thousands of years, interrupted only by the sight of an occasional passing cruise ship like a floating hotel, and a stream of small, heavily-laden *feluccas* sailing by.

"Daniel, may I suggest a topic for another lecture? Abydos. The highlight of our cruise for me, and probably yours too. What about sharing your controversial theories about Abydos?"

"Do you think it would be interesting for the family?"

"If anyone can make it so, you can. Shock them with your honesty about ancient Egypt."

"Let's talk about murder, mass murder," Daniel began. Interest stirred among the seated family in the Lounge. Was murder on their minds, or were they gruesome and ghastly?

"Egyptologists shrink from the subject, but in the earliest dynasties of Egypt, the king died and then people died. Particularly at Abydos, a highlight-stop of our cruise and the setting of countless murders. By that I mean the burial of royal subjects and servants who were forced to accompany a dead king into the afterlife. Egyptologists use the euphemisms 'subsidiary burials' and 'retainer sacrifices', but it was murder of the innocent. Perfect specimens. Young people, at the prime of their lives, killed and buried.

How did they die? They were not buried alive as some old movies suggest. Instead, archaeologists have found their bodies set out in an orderly fashion. None showed signs of mutilation or trauma on their skeletal remains as a result of say smiting their heads with maces in the pharaonic tradition. Some say these people died as a result of cyanide poisoning, others that they were strangled to death. Maybe their executioners borrowed from similar practices in neighbouring civilizations such as Sumeria, that show piercings into the skull cavity to the brain by a sharp instrument, possibly lifting an eye-lid to penetrate the brain, while leaving no trace.

However it happened, the king's retinue and subjects joined him on a one-way journey to the underworld.

I'm talking about First Dynasty pharaohs like King Djer, the biggest culprit of such murders, his tomb buried in the deep sands of Abydos, overlooked by looming cliffs. Around Djer's vast single burial pit chamber with its internal chambers, lay satellite graves, honeycomb rows of cell-like cavities containing the bodies of three hundred and eighteen victims. Men and women. Perfect specimens. Reminding us of the 'unblemished beast sacrifices' of animals.

It was all about religious beliefs, yes, but also about status. You don't have great status in the afterlife if you don't have people under you to obey your every command.

In the Middle Kingdom of Egypt, a thousand years later, priests mistakenly declared the tomb of King Djer to be the tomb of the man-god Osiris, Lord of the Dead, and henceforth it became a site of pilgrimages and the setting for religious passion plays. Yet even earlier, Abydos was seen by the Egyptians as the site of the primary entrance to the underworld.

My controversial theory is this. There existed an earlier funerary god-king before Osiris, and his name was Khentiamentiu, depicted like Osiris as a man swathed in mummiform bandages, whose emblem was a standing jackal-dog. In fact, Osiris later absorbed his predecessor's attributes, which is why Osiris carried the epithet Osiris-Khentiamentiu. And Khentiamentiu was in turn associated with another jackal dog, Wepwawet, the 'Opener of Ways', but let's not get stuck in the weeds of Egyptology. Importantly, ancient Egyptians, and later Greek historians too, insist these god-kings actually existed, ruled in a golden age, and then were buried.

I theorize that Khentiamentiu lived and died and was buried at Abydos, along with the treasures of a man god, in a tomb possibly linked with the legendary entrance to the underworld. In fact, he may even share his tomb with the added burial of a Fourth Dynasty pharaoh Khufu, builder of the Great Pyramid of Giza. A surprising suggestion?

Khufu's remains and treasures have never been found. His Great Pyramid chamber and coffin were found empty. Is it possible that Khufu changed his mind about the role of his pyramid at the last minute, as other pharaohs did, and instead had himself buried in the holiest site in Egypt, Abydos, leaving his empty Great Pyramid as the world's largest memorial cenotaph? You see, no statue has ever been found of king Khufu at Giza, site of his pyramid. Only one small ivory statue of Khufu has ever turned up. In... yes, you guessed it, Abydos!

Perhaps a bit of a stretch, this part of my theory, but a teaser.

Why haven't archaeologists found Khentiamentiu's tomb-of-all tombs?

The singing sands of Abydos are probably to blame. Singing sands? The desert here produces an eerie sound when the wind blows over it, said to be caused by the peculiarly fine, *aeolian* sand. Others say the singing is a ghostly echo of the mourning and jubilation of ancient pilgrims, processions of worshipers who over the centuries reenacted the funeral rites of Osiris.

The sands of Abydos are deep. 'You don't clear it away with a brush', as one archaeologist put it. Ground-penetrating radar hints at other hidden structures, but mainstream Egyptology rejects my theory about Khentiameniu. Maybe, one day..."

Calder Hall tapped his stick on the floor in solitary applause at the end.

"Thank you, Daniel. Maybe one day you'll find the key that will shake up the old Egyptology community."

The *Belle Epoque* paddle wheeler stopped at *Minya* and the group went ashore to visit *Tel El Amarna,* in pursuit of what travel brochures called the 'Amarna Experience'. But the empty plain of Amarna, abandoned after just seven years to the winds and the wolves, or at least the jackal-dogs, was an experience of desolation, a vanished empire of the imagination set in sepia sand, as Daniel described it.

Their Egyptian tour guide on the site swept an arm across the view of the plain.

"Here Pharaoh Akhenaten built his brand new city and worshiped his sole god, Aten, whose symbol was the shining disk of the sun." When that failed to impress the family, he added: "We are standing on the historic plain of Amarna."

"Plain boring, if you ask me," Computer Man said in a mutter.

Calder's family members were not worshipers of the sun. They scowled in the dazzling Amarna heat. Where were images of swan-necked Nefertiti and mad king Akhenaten?

"You will see them in the tombs," the guide pointed.

But where were the palaces and sun temples? Where was the city?

Tomb images of Akhenaten and Nefertiti

On the following morning, the stringed turquoise necklace of their cruise itinerary snapped and the gems scattered around the decks of *Belle Epoque* like the shock of a jewel robbery.

The old man Calder Hall, host of their cruise, had gone missing.

News flew around the boat.

The vessel had slipped its mooring early in the morning before the passengers stirred and Calder had not been missed until later in the day. Perhaps the old man had slept in after a stirring folkloric dancing show on board that night, performed by the crew, and the drinking that had continued later.

At least that was what people assumed.

Now the old man was gone.

But how could he disappear?

The lawyer Hyman Robbins broke the news to Daniel on a flying visit to their cabin, the young Egyptian filmmaker in tow, clutching her camcorder.

CHAPTER 6
The dig begins

"What do you want to do?" Legal Suit said to Daniel.
"Do?"
"You're in charge."
"Of?"
"The investigation."
"Ah, yes. Investigation. We must investigate. I think the boat should be searched from stem to stern."
"We've done that."
"Then do it again. More thoroughly this time. Calder's playing a game, but I hardly think he'd jump overboard in the spirit of it. No, he's found a secret hiding place somewhere and won't reappear until we've found his killer."
"Then you think - "
"We're playing a game, right?"
The lawyer gulped.
"How do I put this? It's not the best time to break it to you, but this is not entirely a game. In fact, not a game at all. The only game was letting you believe that this was to be a mock murder cruise. My client's misdirection. He wanted you to discover the truth for yourself. Mr Hall liked putting people into situations, as I tried to warn you."
A gravitational pull took hold of Daniel's body. It felt as if the *Belle Epoque* had suddenly gone into reverse, back-paddling furiously.
"So it's real and not some reality production."
The *Belle Epoque* kept going straight ahead, while Daniel's mind went on lurching.
"It's reality, and yes, it could be defined as quite a production," the lawyer said.

"I told you nobody seemed to be acting," Kate said in a murmur to Daniel.

"Calder's last great production," Daniel said.

"You might say that," Legal Suit said.

"And now he's gone missing?"

"Yes. So what procedural steps do you wish to take?"

"I suppose we should talk to the family."

"But should we not return to our last stop? In case Mr Hall got off the boat unobserved, perhaps in the quiet hours? Or fell overboard?"

If Calder had fallen into the River Nile he could be miles downstream by now. Should they turn around and start combing the river?

It sounded futile to Daniel.

"First we bring the family into this."

"Which of you was the last one to see Calder last night?" Daniel said.

The family, assembled in the Lounge, stood around in a defensive semi-circle.

Nobody responded.

"C'mon Craig. We heard Dad ask you to help him with his computer last night," the elder sister said.

"Okay, I admit. I saw him late last night."

Computer Man.

"I went with him to his suite. He was having computer problems, his programmes and apps crashing. I said it was late and I'd take his machine back to my cabin to look at, but Dad stuck to his rules. No access to computers or phones, except his. He made me fix the problem while he breathed down my neck. It didn't take me long."

"How long? What time did you leave his suite?"

"Around midnight. He was fine when I left him."

"You would say that," Big Brother said in an accusing tone. "But why would you do such a dumb thing to him?"

"Maybe he's in debt again and wanted to fast track his inheritance, if he's stupid enough to think he's getting one," a sister suggested.

"Yes," the other agreed. "Maybe he hasn't been able to hack any bank accounts lately. He's prison population, our baby brother."

"At least I shared some of it with you, when you two needed money."

"Shared what wasn't yours."

"Why would I do anything to Dad, especially when you heard him ask me to go to his cabin to fix his computer?"

"You're brazen, like all cons."

But where was the motive to harm the father?

The Will? Computer Man's behaviour had not been that of someone expecting, or deserving, an inheritance. He'd ignored the onboard lectures his father had arranged for the family, blatantly displaying a total lack of interest in proceedings.

Was it revenge that drove him to it? Anger at his father? 'Something doesn't quite click,' Daniel thought.

His next step would be to visit the possible scene of the crime.

The old man's luxury suite.

Legal Suit and camera-girl accompanied him. Wooden-framed picture windows in the sumptuous suite gave panoramic views of the Nile ahead and challenged the notion of a death scene. 'Jack' the jackal-dog walking stick was still here, propped against an antique table, standing guard over the suite, so the old man hadn't slipped ashore. He would never have gone anywhere without his stick.

The bed lay unused.

A thumbed copy of *Death on the Nile* sat on his bedside table. Bottles of gin, whisky and a selection of fine ports stood on a silver tray on a dresser. The old man's golden laptop computer sat open on an antique desk. Wouldn't Calder have closed the lid if he'd finished with it? Maybe.

Daniel wondered about the computer and what it might tell. Calder was a dying man. He might have fallen prey to depression and revealed something.

Daniel started up the machine.

"A suicide note, I wonder?" he said.

The computer flashed into life and asked for a password.

"Can't get in. Maybe a dead end anyway. The old man was enjoying himself far too much on the *Belle Epoque.*"

Calder had also been keen to fulfill his dream of reaching Abydos and then going on to the destination of Aswan and completing a last 'linear progression' up the Nile - although he probably guessed he would never make it all the way.

There was no sign of a struggle or disturbance in the suite, let alone blood.

What next?

"Okay, we'd better turn the boat around now and head back to the other possible scene of the crime. The riverside mooring where he was last seen," Daniel said.

"I'll inform the Boat Manager," Legal Suit said.

An old man's body had been found on the riverbank, enquiries by the Boat Manager discovered from local villagers. Had he been in the water? A little hard to tell. He was dry after lying there in the heat of the day. Perhaps somebody had spotted the body and dragged it ashore, looking for money.

Daniel, the lawyer and the filmmaker Mayet joined the
ship's doctor, a Coptic Egyptian, in the boat's white
medical clinic area where the body lay under a sheet on
an examination table, hidden behind a screen.
"He did not drown," the doctor explained. "He was
clubbed to death with something blunt. See, here." The
doctor pulled back the sheet. Daniel had been up close
and personal with ancient Egyptian mummies, so death
no longer frightened him, yet it was a relief not to be
met by the bloodied face of the dead man. Instead, the
sponsor of archaeology had been turned onto his
stomach to display his back and a view of multiple
blows to the old man's bald crown, back of the head,
neck and spine.
Blows had rained down on him.
A scene of a wall carving flashed into Daniel's mind of a
pharaoh clubbing his enemies to death, but if this had
been the work of a single executioner then he must have
struck in an unhinged fury that seemed excessive.
Multiple attackers?
Daniel pictured a Julius-Caesar style execution with the
whole family, like a ring of conspirators, raining blows
on Calder's head and body.
Was it possible?
A joint murder?
A rare moment of family togetherness?
Mystifying.
"What now?" the lawyer said.
"There's no playing around any longer. Call in the police
and call off this cruise."
"That's not in the agreement." The lawyer shook his
head. "You are in charge of the investigation, as
stipulated, but I am enforcing the terms of the
agreement solemnly drawn up with everybody on board
and I will not be neglecting my deceased client's
instructions. Mr Hall intended the cruise to complete its
journey up the Nile, come what may. And that is
precisely what we shall do. Therefore nobody must leave

the cruise and the cruise must continue as planned. We are just at the beginning."
Legal Suit.
It might have sounded like a bizarre idea to honour a dead man's cruise itinerary, but not so peculiar to an Egyptologist like Daniel. After all, mummies of ancient Egypt's wealthy classes customarily embarked on *post mortem* journeys by boat along the Nile. They made a pilgrimage to the holy site at Abydos, traditionally believed to be the burial ground of the god Osiris, Lord of the Underworld and Judge of the Dead, before being returned to their home city for final burial.
"But what about the body?" he said.
"We have a spare chill room, largely empty with such a small passenger list on the cruise," the doctor said.
"We continue, as normally as possible," Legal Suit said. "In fact, tomorrow morning I am bound to read out the first part of my deceased client's Will." How smoothly the lawyer's description of Calder Hall slipped from 'client' to 'deceased client'.
"You're going through with this? All the way?"
"As indeed you must, too, in order to receive the full sum of your fee, according to the agreement we struck."

Bad Cop Uncle Bryan cornered Daniel on deck.
"Do you know what you're doing, Mister Archaeology Excavator? I thought you might be walking around with a shovel."
The descriptor made Daniel feel he should be wearing a hard hat.
Ex-cop Uncle Bryan clearly thought as a former detective he was the experienced one who should be put in charge of the investigation.
"We don't often use shovels in archaeology. Mostly a small, flat trowel," Daniel said in reply.
The tight skin over Uncle Bryan's cheeks grew tighter.

"Have you made a proper investigation of the crime scene? Gone over my brother's suite and collected all the evidence?"

"Brushed the place over with powder for fingerprints? No. We prefer using brushes to dust off dirt in archaeology."

"A crime scene can tell you a lot, if you know what you're looking for. You want some tips?"

"About who did it, sure."

"About doing your job. Maybe you should step aside and let a pro head up the investigation."

"I'm afraid you're disqualified."

"What have they been telling you about me? I was wrongly discharged."

"You're disqualified because you are a member of the family and must be seen as one of the suspects."

The grizzled man laughed with an unpleasant wheeze. "So we're all suspects! How do you know some crew member didn't do it?"

"Do you know how important the tourist trade is to Egyptians, how much they've suffered without tourism in the past?" Daniel said. "The crew nearly kissed us all when we came on board. No, I don't think this crew is going to be killing anybody."

"You think I'm a suspect? You think a good cop is going to do a stupid stunt like kill someone in a lock-up?"

"Maybe not a good cop. I've been put in charge. Your brother was quite specific about it."

"I hope you've secured the crime scene. Once it's tampered with it's never the same."

That was true of archaeology too, Daniel thought. Archaeology was a destructive profession. Once you'd dug up and disturbed a site, it stopped telling you things.

"I haven't put crime scene tape around the suite, if what's what you mean, but yes, the suite is now off limits."

"Any sign of forced entry?"

"The door was unlocked at the time."
"Anything in his trash bin? In his bathroom?"
"Bathroom?"
"Clues. Wet towels, cloths, signs of a clean up? Was the toilet seat left up?"
"What does that prove?"
"Old guys leak a lot. We tend to leave the seat up all the time. So if the seat's down, a lady might have used it. Or ladies. We'd all been drinking a lot. Did you even notice?"
"Thanks, but I'm the one supposed to be asking questions."
"About that. When are you going to start proper Investigative interviews?"
"We try not to rush things in archaeology."
"I haven't noticed you doing any surveillance, either. Secretly hiding and watching suspects for suspicious behaviour."
"Then I've been successful."
Uncle Bryan apparently expected Daniel to go behind potted palms and aspidistras in a surveillance operation.
"You gotta build a case, Buddy."
Archaeologists didn't build cases, they built narratives about people and mythologies of the past, Daniel thought, but it was a fine point of difference Uncle Bryan might not appreciate.

THE VIDEOCAM SHOWS THE FACE OF THE YOUNGEST MEMBER OF THE FAMILY IN CLOSE-UP. HE RESENTS THE SCRUTINY.

"I wasn't the last one of us to see my father alive. Somebody else was. The one who killed him. Just because I went to Dad's cabin late in the night doesn't prove anything. I was helping him, more

than the others ever did. What about my big
brother? He was always throwing his weight around.
Or my weird and creepy sisters who sit there all day
with their balls of knitting wool and needles going
clickety clack. Mixing colours like witches stirring
potions.
If I hadn't discovered computer games as a kid, my
family would have driven me bat-shit crazy. But you
can't dump my father's death on me."

THE VIDEOCAM CAPTURES A LARGE MAN WHO FILLS
A DECKCHAIR AS WELL AS THE LENS.

 "What has little brother been telling you? The one
whose favourite words as a kid were always: "I didn't
do it! It wasn't me!" It usually was.
Or my craft-loving sisters that my father
underestimates. They've got clever fingers, but
they're also manipulative. I wouldn't put it past
them to do something.
Two of them could have pulled it off together and I
can't really blame them for hating him, the way he
treated them.
The way he treated all of us.
No, that doesn't mean I hated him enough to kill
him. But as the eldest, I suppose I should have done
more to protect the old man. From us."

THE VIDEO CAM SHOWS TWO WOMEN, SISTERS,
ENGAGED IN MAKING A BALL FROM A SKEIN OF
BLACK WOOL, USING THE ONE'S SPLAYED HANDS
AND THUMB AS A WINDING ARM. THEY PAUSE
MOMENTARILY TO SPEAK TO THE CAMERA.

"It doesn't make a lot of sense to kill our father –"

"– not if we're supposed to be on this cruise to make a good impression on him. So he'd put us in his wool –"
"– Will, she meant."
"Tragic business."
"Awful. But men can be violent. Our brothers have a lot of anger issues.
We never did impress our father and I don't think we succeeded on this cruise. But we didn't kill him."

THE VIDEOCAM INTERROGATES THE TIGHT, ANGRY FEATURES OF A GRIZZLED MAN. HE GLARES DOWN THE LENS.

"That tomb digger guy! He's an investigator without a clue. And you know what? He's not going to find one either. You don't get to understand crime investigation by watching CIS or remakes of Agatha Christie murders. Death on the Nile? Ha Ha. I'll tell you about a death. That Egyptologist is going to kill this investigation. Why hasn't he hauled everybody aside for questioning, one at a time? Does he even know the techniques of interviewing suspects? People are tricky, slippery things. They don't just lie there under your magnifying glass."

THE VIDEOCAM SEES EGYPTOLOGIST DANIEL CANE PACING THE CONFINES OF THE SMALL ON-BOARD LIBRARY,
THE CAMERA PANS WITH HIM.

"So here it is, the last production of Calder Hall. I suppose I should be grilling the family for clues - creating some dramatic Interrogation scenes for your camera. Following the standard criminal investigation process we see in movies. But to me

that feels like taking the artefact out of its context before I've properly studied or recorded it within its context - and that context here is the family. I think that in forming my impressions I should look at them *where they are* in their family strata, observing the group dynamics rather than putting them in a lab for microscopic study.
I don't think I was hired to turn this into a police procedural story.
If I was, then they're going to be as disappointed as Uncle Bryan."

Nile village

CHAPTER 7
A Malignant Will

Before the afternoon break, Daniel took himself to his favourite thinking place above a churning paddle wheel. The turn of the wheel seemed to impel his thinking and encourage a sense of progress.

Today the rotating paddles in the water produced a different sound to Daniel's ear.

Shit, shit, shit.

Who'd have picked the father to be a victim, and so early?

He leaned against a rail and gazed out at a riverbank view of passing farmland where workers toiled at their plots. Not much in rural Egypt had changed over the centuries. Donkeys trotted along the bank, dwarfed by sheaves of watercress on their backs. A *fellaheen* raised water to his irrigation canal. Some farmer still used a *shaduf,* an ancient Egyptian invention involving a bucket hinged on a lengthy pole to lever up water, but this one used a cow to turn a vertical water wheel, a kind of paddle wheel with clay pots strapped to the outside rim that scooped up water and deposited it in gushes at a higher level, a device introduced in the Roman period.

Yet another turning paddle wheel, Daniel thought, like a sort of mechanized bucket brigade.

Splash, splash, spash.

For some reason he pictured the dead man's family working in unison in a bucket brigade, the bedeviling idea returning that they had all somehow combined to club him to death, each armed with a weapon.

Bash, bash, bash.

Wheels within wheels turned in Daniel's brain.

Why kill the old man at all?

THE VIDEO STREAM FINDS EGYPTOLOGIST DANIEL CANE BACK IN THE LIBRARY OF THE *BELLE EPOQUE,* ADDRESSING THE CAMERA.

"Shocking fact has overtaken fiction. What was presented to me as an entertaining mystery game has suddenly turned into a very deadly one. My host and employer, and the patriarch of the family, has turned out to be an unexpected victim.
Egyptology is all about death. Death was the testator that bequeathed us our knowledge of the ancient Egyptians, and did so in a profusion and richness unmatched by any other ancient civilization.
But death is a shock in the here and now. No less for me. Yet I don't see much grieving going on here. There are none of those scenes of a family holding up their arms to the skies in mourning that we see painted on the walls of tombs, no hired female mourners wailing and throwing the dust of anguish onto their hair. This group is more like vultures circling, hungry to swoop and gorge on a carcass.

Death in Egypt

Morning coffees and teas served in the Lounge was more
like a wake.
If this was not a contrived murder mystery, then it
followed the tropes.
A death, followed by a Reading of the Will to an
undeserving, assembled family. The family and the
lawyer sat in a semi-circle of soft chairs and couches.
Kate sat aside.
Mayet, the Egyptian girl, positioned herself to record
events on her camcorder.
It was amazing how quickly she blended into the
scenery, in spite of her jaunty beret.
Legal Suit, Hyman Robbins, addressed them, opening
an envelope with none of the fumbling that occurred at
academy awards ceremonies.
"The Last Will and Testament of Calder Hall..." he
announced, then paused to scan the standard legalese.
"I won't hold you in suspense with the preliminaries
about the Executor... *me*... and about *my* total powers
as the Executor, etcetera... I'll move to the Disposition of
the Estate." He frowned here. "But a note of warning."
He shifted uncomfortably in his chair. "This document
breaks with the pattern by including some informal
opening statements. It's an address by Calder Hall to
you all."
Hyman Robbins looked over his reading glasses at them,
cleared his throat and read out his dead client's words:-

"I had thought of opening this preliminary statement to
you, my surviving family, with six words.
Go to hell, all of you!

Or maybe, more colourfully, opening with a
pronouncement of an ancient Egyptian curse...

May you all lose your earthly positions and honors.

Daniel found himself warming to the now cold Calder Hall.

He gave an involuntary chuckle, which made him rattle his coffee cup in its saucer. Kate bumped his knee and frowned in disapproval. The old patriarch's broadside hardly surprised the family.

Perhaps they expected contempt from him.

But a curse?

Calder Hall clearly guessed he was going to die some time along this cruise and was unlikely to reach the end, Daniel thought, though he may not have quite expected his own murder.

Legal Suit continued the reading.

"However, I can't take it all with me as they say, unlike my beloved Egyptian pharaohs, who buried their riches in tombs alongside their mummies. So here is my Will... or the first part of it." The lawyer paused for dramatic effect. "Who receives inheritance in the Estate?

Only ONE, to be named in a second reading of a codicil at the end of the cruise. Only ONE party shall receive benefits from my estate - the entire inheritance - effective from the final day of the cruise. However, should the undisclosed beneficiary fail to survive to the last day of the cruise, as a result of some unforeseen circumstance, then the family shall all share EQUALLY in the inheritance. Note, if any beneficiary under this Will contests any of the provisions of this Will, then each and all such persons shall not be entitled to any devises, legacies or benefits under this Will or codicil hereto...

Furthermore, the cruise must go on, whatever occurs, as the Captain and crew have been instructed. If you do

not reach Aswan on the due date, the provisions of Distribution will be cancelled and the entire estate awarded to archaeology."
One member would receive ALL of the estate?
'Interesting twist,' Daniel thought.
Also alarming.
Fail to survive to the last day of the cruise, as a result of some unforeseen circumstance?
Ominous.
The father planned to set the family at each other's throats. If they truly were as vile as the dead man suggested, then this reading of the Will could turn the gracious *Belle Epoque* into a gladiatorial arena.
"Only one to inherit? This is a bad joke, right?" Big Brother said.
"*One*?" the close-knit sisters said as one, dropping their knitting.
The family swung accusing looks at each other. All except Computer Man, who sat, disinterested as always, legs crossed as if to accentuate the absence of his confiscated laptop that he had so compulsively fiddled with earlier. Maybe it was resignation in his attitude. If only *one* party would inherit from the father, it wouldn't be him.
Who was the 'chosen' one?
The Sisterhood fixed their stare on the bulk of Big Brother.
"It's you, isn't it, Leo," the elder sister said accusingly to the brother. "That's right - give it all to the eldest male!"
"Yay, go the patriarchy!" the other sister cheered caustically.
A potential beneficiary might have shown satisfaction at being tipped by his siblings as a favoured one, but Big Brother looked as if he'd been fingered and was uncomfortable about taking the heat, despite the air-conditioned surroundings of the boat Lounge. He used a blunt finger to loosen his collar.

"That's bull. Dad had no time for me, and if he was just going to follow a traditional form of choosing the eldest son, then why drag all of us here to this goddamned place?"
Daniel couldn't resist making a dig.
"Maybe it's another hidden legacy," he said. "An educational experience to pass on his love of ancient Egypt to you all."
If it was a legacy, then it was not one they valued.
"Thanks Dad –" the sisters addressed the absent father loudly.
"– for nothing!"
"We've got the History Channel at home if we wanted ancient history," Big Brother said.
"You won't find too much of it there," Daniel said.
"Ancient Aliens..?"
Was this the start of more mayhem?
Daniel still had to address the death of the father - and the sight of Bad Cop Uncle Bryan glowering from his chair challenged him.

After the reading of the Will, Daniel stood up.
Big Brother snorted.
"You think we're going to sit here and listen to a lecture on ancient history? We don't have to humour the old man any more."
"Not a lecture," Daniel said. "But you may want to listen to what I have to say. I know how your father died."
That got their attention.
Everybody's.
Including Computer Man's.
And especially Bad Cop's.
"You know?" the sisters said.
"We all know how he died," Bad Cop said in a weary voice. "The doctor's report said he got hit on the head."

"Yes," Daniel said, "and on the back of the head and on the neck and along the spine. A thicket of clubs falling on him one after the other," he said, sweeping them in a glance.

"You think we ganged up on our father?" the Sisterhood said.

"It did occur to me, I must be honest," Daniel said. 1q

"We're women. Women don't club people to death."

"No? Nefertiti did. But I think there's another explanation."

"Please continue," Legal Suit said.

"Those club wounds on Calder Hall's body are the result of bludgeoning caused by rotating paddle wheels, striking his body one after another. It must have happened when the boat left the mooring early yesterday. The paddle wheel sucked him underneath."

"Then that's how he died," Computer Man said.

"Not necessarily. One of those blows, the initial deadly one, comes from his killer, I believe. That's why your father didn't drown. He must have been dead before he hit the water. Struck on the head with a heavy object, which I now suspect, after checking the suite's liquor bar inventory, was a missing bottle of vintage tawny port. His body was then tipped over the bow into the water, probably in the expectation that it would float away in the current. But somehow his body snagged under a paddle wheel where it took a sustained beating in the morning."

"A missing bottle of port doesn't prove anything," Computer Man said.

"The kid's right. A cabin cleaner could have taken the bottle," Uncle Bryan added.

"Muslims don't drink," Daniel said.

"But how can you prove foul play if he had so many bangs on him?"

"He didn't drown, remember."

"He may have banged his head and died on the way down as he fell overboard somehow," Computer Man said.

"Admittedly, yes, it would be hard to prove my theory. That's why whoever performed the deed, walks free for now. They're among us. But this is a lock-up, luxurious as it is, so they're not going anywhere."

"So what are we supposed to do, carry on paddling up the river as if nothing's happened?" Big Brother said.

Legal Suit harked back to the terms and conditions.

"The rules still apply. The cruise must continue, come what may. Or nobody inherits."

"I've got a question for you, Mr Egyptologist," Big Brother said. "How well did you know our father?"

"Know?"

"Were you confidants? We know the lawyer Hyman Robbins. He's been the family lawyer for decades and our father's guarded confidant, but why are you here?"

"I'm a guest Egyptologist."

"Our father bankrolled Egyptology. He must have known plenty of Egyptologists, many who'd worked with him. He was also a man who never did things by accident. Why choose you? Maybe you know what was going on in his mind because Hyman Robbins here certainly won't tell us. So we ask again, how well did you know him?"

"I met him once at a conference. Before he hired me for the cruise. Maybe you should be asking how well he knew you. Too well maybe? Or enough to know that somebody here, the lucky one who gets the pharaoh's treasure, if he or she survives the cruise, possesses some claim to virtue the rest of you don't?"

Daniel, the lawyer, and Kate, left the Lounge.

The family remained, silent, in a state of bemusement

On an impulse, Daniel stopped at the door to linger outside.

"You go on," he said.

"You're going to eavesdrop?" Kate said.

"I told you it's not beyond me."

"You're supposed to be playing detective, not spy."

He placed a finger to his lips.

The two left.

Daniel flattened himself against a paneled wall to listen. Nothing. The soft chug of the steam engine vibrated through the vessel's interior. Was it drowning out their voices?

No, they'd been stunned into silence.

Somebody spoke.

Computer Man's voice.

"You know what? I've got a suggestion, a solution that might stop us all squabbling for hundreds of miles. We've got a lawyer on board. Let's draw up an agreement that whichever family member gets named as the sole heir at the end of the cruise they will waive their right and agree to share the inheritance equally among all of us."

Desolate emptiness ensued like the sound of crickets at night.

Stupefaction at the simplicity of the suggestion? Daniel wondered.

Not for long.

"There you go again, splashing around money that isn't yours to give," a sister said.

"Think about it. Doesn't it sound fair?" the young brother said.

"Not a bad suggestion, Kid," Bad Cop said.

"Easy for you to say," Big Brother said.

"Yes, who thinks you're even in the running?"

"Little brother is scheming – "

"– as always," the Sisterhood said.

What kind of family was this? Were they that greedy? Evidently this family didn't do fair. It was eminently fair in Daniel's view, in fact it had a surprising touch of reasonableness, even generosity.

Silence again.

Daniel heard the scrape of a chair.
They were coming out.
He left.

VIDEOCAM CAPTURES DANIEL LOOKING PENSIVE, NOT ENTIRELY PLEASED WITH HIMSELF. HE IS ON DECK FROWNING IN THE BRIGHT LIGHT, LISTENING TO THE REGULAR BEAT OF THE PADDLE WHEEL.

(Young Female voice, off camera, speaks with a faint Arabic accent:)

"What are you thinking and feeling, Daniel? Are you satisfied with your work on the investigation?

"I'm satisfied with my hunch about the paddle wheel blows, but my thoughts are still spinning. I still don't understand a lot of things. Who killed the father? Why? Why so early on in the cruise?
Do I, as an Egyptologist and archaeologist, have special tools that I can bring to the investigation?
Digging, sifting the clues, establishing context, dating and interpreting them, classifying them, analysing, deciphering and preserving them, recording every steps of the progress, which you are apparently doing for me on camera...
In archaeology, artefacts emerge in front of your eyes and you can see them. The detective can't be sure if what he's looking at is a clue. Anything around him could be a clue.
I suppose my next step is to get underneath the hidden layers of the suspects. But instead of interrogating them one on one, I might try a different approach. After dinner tonight..."

River Nile, passing scenery

CHAPTER 8
Quiz Night

It was a muted dinner in the dining saloon, with only murmured conversation, accompanied by the clink and tinkle of silver cutlery on fine bone china.

It was time to dig beneath the surface layers, Daniel thought. You had to break ground to find the truth.

The family had chosen separate tables, he noted. No togetherness in grief tonight.

Daniel stood.

"Your attention, please, diners. Our Nile cruise itinerary declares an after dinner entertainment this evening. It's Quiz Night!" He looked around with a wan smile. The family looked back appalled. They hadn't signed up for party games, in spite of Calder Hall's couching the cruise to Daniel as a mock murder mystery. "Quiz Night suggests trivia questions, or general knowledge, but I want to do something more specific. I want to quiz you about your relationship with your father.

Instead of interrogating each of you, tied to a chair under a naked light bulb, we'll do this in a more comfortable setting, right here, over glasses of vintage port, which I see is now being served." Liveried stewards spread through the dining saloon filling Edwardian style glasses.

"I want to ask each of you: what was your relationship with your father?"

They took shelter behind their ports.

"Do I have to nominate a family member? Come on now, who's first? You don't have to get up on your feet."

Eyes avoided his.

Big Brother put down his port.

"As the eldest son, I suppose I should take the lead."

That got a stare, but tension eased around the saloon.

Big Brother looked a little damp, fearful.

Not of Daniel, or the quiz, it appeared, but of his audience, the attentive family, a fear which he betrayed through uneasy, sidelong glances.

He was afraid of his own family.

Was it perilous to be popular, to make yourself look like the best prospect for an inheritance?

Was this family not only greedy, but dangerously so, and did Big Brother fear that he might put a target on his back? If only one in the room could inherit from the father, then this could become an elimination game where the strongest candidate got knocked out first.

"My father called me a waste of space. Large space," the big man said. He tried to soften things with a smile. "I was the only child for seven years, yet never felt like the favourite in all that time. And that situation didn't change when the others came along. My father, the big time producer, only had time for his other productions, and for this place he poured money into, Egypt. Or the ancient relics of it. I became rebellious, crossed him constantly, dropped out of college, spent my allowance on drink, disappointed him in every way. So no, my chances of being the sole heir to my father's estate are a lot slimmer than I am."

Big Brother was damning his own prospects.

"Then what if I suggested you killed your father?" Daniel put it to him.

"Are you? I'd say he was dying anyway. Why kill my father? I didn't know before he died that he was thinking of choosing only one to inherit. None of us did."

True enough.

The eldest of the two close-knit sisters put down her glass.

"Okay, I think I speak for my sister here too –"

"You usually do," Computer Man said.

" – when I say that our father had contempt for his daughters. He thought of us as spinsters, literally, homebody material more interested in craft than careers. He made us feel we were failures. We could never remember anything about ancient history, he said. But he was the typical patriarchal rich man who probably never expected anything of us anyway."

"And wasn't disappointed," Computer Man muttered into his glass.

"Did you or your sister, or both of you, get rid of your father?" Daniel said.

"Knock our father on the head and heave him overboard? We're more subtle than that, in spite of what our father thought of us."

"Thank you. So far you've all made convincing cases for being left out of the Will."

"I've got something to say." Bad Cop spoke up. "I've never heard anything like this in all my years on the force. You call this an investigative interview? Is this how you're going to dig up the perpetrator? You just can't do community interviews."

"Yet here we are," Daniel said. "So what about you and your brother?"

"Look, he had a grudge against me all his life."

"And you had a grudge against him for being rich," a Sister piped up.

"A rich guy who saw me as police hack," Uncle Bryan said.

"You mean as a cop turned bad who got thrown out of the force for using excessive violence?" the other sister added.

Bad Cop glared at the two sisters as if he was on the verge of throwing an Edwardian glass at them.

"I can top that," Computer Man said. "I disappointed my father most of all. I ended up in prison for computer fraud. I hacked people's accounts, including my father's."

Maybe they had tongues marked with the feather of truth, too, Daniel thought.

They were all being brutally honest in discounting themselves.

"This dream cruise has turned out to be a game after all. A deadly game," Kate said as she lay beside him in their antique brass bed in their cabin while the *Belle Epoque* lay moored overnight at Asyut. "What are you thinking?"

"I'm thinking of the old man lying dead on board with us, like one of those ancient Egyptian mummies in their wrappings as they made their ritual *post mortem* voyage by river to the holy city of Abydos."

"That's depressing."

"What's even more depressing is the fact that I'm not making much progress. Maybe archaeologists and detectives are in sister professions, but you can unearth a lot more with a trowel."

"You were clever about the paddles."

"But I'm still missing something."

"Like the identity of the murderer, maybe? Look, I know they're not a loving or loveable family, but honestly, do you really think one of them did it?"

"I honestly do."

"Okay, then tell me the truth, who's your chief suspect?"

"I honestly don't know. Maybe I'm out of my depth. I'm steering this investigation in the wrong direction, into the shallows, and I've hit the bottom of the river where I'm stuck, high and dry."

"That's a lot of riverboat metaphors."

"It's the truth about how I feel."

"Maybe this new side of you is not such a bad thing, Daniel. This new streak of honesty. I like hearing about a man's feelings. I feel you're opening up and we're getting closer."

"We could get even closer," he suggested.

Suggestively.

She chuckled and tickled him.

What was it about death, sex and eternity?

It was an eight-hour sail to their next stop of Sohag.
Eight hours of uninterrupted cruising up the Nile.
And pondering.
Maybe the constant movement of travel would help
move his investigation forward.
That morning Daniel was morosely deliberating the
situation over a breakfast of 'Eggs Benedict served with
mushrooms sautéed in butter and basil', when Legal
Suit dropped in to join them at their table, a glass of
orange juice in hand.
"How was your exploratory dig for information last
night?" he said. "Fruitful, I trust." Was he expecting a
progress report?
Daniel couldn't lie.
"It turned out to be a quiz without answers," he said. "It
didn't sound to me as any of them should expect to
inherit from their father. Surely, as his confidant, you
know something."
"I am still in a privileged position and I take my duty
seriously. Therefore I am not at liberty to divulge
anything."
A man of great probity and one with a deep keel. Hyman
Robbins was not swayed by events. This was not a man
driven by the moral laws of the Ten Commandments:
Thou shalt not kill thy rich and neglectful father
Thou shalt not covet thy greedy siblings share of the
inheritance.
Thou salt not steal by hacking thy father's account.
Thou shalt honor thy quirky father...
Instead, Hyman Robbins was governed by the law of
contract, and he would observe the letter of the law to
the end.

Daniel left Kate on the upper deck to read her book on
Egyptian mythology. He revisited his thinking place.

The splashing paddle wheel and the rural landscape of eternal Egypt only alarmed him today as if answers were passing him by, along with time.

Only one more stop overnight in Sohag and then they would be at Abydos.

He wondered if Calder Hall, stiffening like a mummy in the boat's cool room, sensed that he was drawing closer to his beloved archaeological site of Abydos, the *post-mortem* destination of pilgrims past?

Should they go ashore and make a site visit?

Why not?

Daniel longed to see Abydos again for numerous reasons.

First, his own curiosity about Abydos had never been satisfied. And it seemed like an act of respect to his employer to carry on his pilgrimage. Kate would enjoy the beautiful artwork of Seti's temple and the family of the dead man needed a break. They'd been pacing around the boat looking as restless as caged animals, all the while keeping a wary look over their shoulders. The *Belle Epoque* was changing from a luxurious cruise boat into an ancient Egyptian funerary barque, Daniel thought.

A stretch of the legs might help everyone.

He attended the morning tea and coffee with Kate, but the family feared another quizzing. The place was empty.

Only Legal Suit and Mayet came.

The rest of the morning and lunch went by in a blur of contemplation, as did the afternoon break where Daniel was the only one to turn up this time. Kate had taken a nap in the cabin.

Dusk was settling on the Nile when he paid another private visit to Calder's suite. Nothing had been touched, by his request.

The sharp nose of the jackal-dog walking stick challenged him as he entered and closed the cabin door.

"Do you know something, Jack?"

He picked up the mobility aid and gave the jackal-dog's head a swing like a seven iron at a par three golf hole.

Then he put it back against a chair and wandered around the suite.

Something said by somebody at the quiz night was stirring in his brain.

The golden computer, still lying open at the antique desk, caught his eye.

The computer.

Was that it?

Ideas collected other ideas like jars in a *felaheen's* water wheel.

Daniel delayed the serving of dinner.

The family, gathered in the Dining Saloon, muttered.

He went out in front.

"According to our cruise itinerary, tonight was supposed to be a Black and White Party. Everybody was meant to dress up in formal black and white. We haven't, but let's not waste the theme. I am going to give you some truth tonight. In black and white. I will tell you who killed Calder Hall."

That stopped the grumbling over the late dinner.

He let the impact set in.

"I recall the eldest son's remark last night. He said:

"Why kill my father? I didn't know before he died that he was thinking of choosing only one to inherit. None of us did."

The family turned stares on Big Brother.

"You think I did it?" he said.

"You raised an interesting point," Daniel went on. "Why kill a dying man? Or more significantly, why kill Calder Hall *before* you heard he planned to limit the inheritance to one beneficiary? None of you knew, you said. But was that in fact true?

It was as if someone knew the process and status of Calder's private deliberations on his Will and wanted to head off something before Calder could put a drastic change into effect. How did they know?"

He glanced in the direction of Computer Man.

"I recall the computer loving member of your family confessing that he disappointed his father most of all. He ended up in prison for computer fraud. He hacked people's accounts, including his father's. Then I recalled how wedded he was to his laptop at the start of our cruise. He was back in the hacking business and his locked up computer will show the evidence. He hacked his father's computer in search of clues about how the old man was thinking. Another giveaway? Calder's computer. His apps and programs had begun to crash. It's one of the warning signs that a computer has been hacked. That's why Calder asked his son to look at his computer in his suite and his son agreed, brazenly taking advantage of the opportunity to kill his father with a now missing bottle of port, before tossing him overboard. He was running out of time and he had to act because his chances of inheriting in the will looked hopeless. That accounts for his sudden burst of magnanimity, which I happened to overhear, his suggestion that you draw up an agreement that whichever family member was named as the sole heir at the end of the cruise, they would waive their right and agree to share the inheritance equally among all. It was the only way to cover all bases, but he had to stop his father in his tracks. The proof of his hacking ways will be there for an expert to prove when this cruise is over. Computer Man didn't argue.

He scraped back his chair and knocked it over, sending it crashing to the Dining Saloon floor.

He bolted for the doors.

Daniel was already springing after him.

"How far do you think you can get?"

The son disappeared out of the door as the Dining Saloon broke into uproar.

Computer Man fled down a companionway to a flight of steps with a curved wooden railing and disappeared. He was heading for the floodlit promenade deck.

Daniel pounded after him.

Taking two steps at a time, he emerged on the deck to hear the drum of running footsteps.

Computer man was sprinting down the promenade deck.

It wasn't going to get him far.

Computer Man glanced back over his shoulder, saw Daniel closing and clambered up the deck rail.

He reached the top, paused, then sprang out into the darkness and hit the Nile with a sharp splash, then vanished.

Legal Suit and Bad Cop came running up.

"He's jumped ship," Daniel said. "Going on the run. He won't find it easy getting out of the country with his passport still on board."

"You let him get away?" Bad Cop said, appalled. "Stop him!"

"You want me to dive in and search the inky black waters of the Nile? It's your nephew, so please, go ahead."

"You would never have made a policeman, Buddy!"

The death dogs of Abydos

CHAPTER 9
Post mortem pilgrimage

They travelled in two vehicles to the desert plain of
Abydos, embayed in the distance by mountain cliffs -
the burial ground of Egypt's earliest royalty and the site
of temples built by later pharaohs Seti and Rameses the
Great.

The mummified dead from all over Egypt came on *post
mortem* journeys of pilgrimage to this burial ground of
the god Osiris - and also of Khentiamentiu and
Wepwawet, if Daniel was right.

Daniel thought of Calder Hall's fondness for this place
and pictured the old man's *ka*-spirit shuffling along,
jackal-dog walking stick in hand, haunting the
exquisitely decorated seven sanctuaries and two
hypostyle halls of the temple of Seti as the visitors
passed through them, trailing the murmuring voice of a
local Egyptian tour guide.

The temple of Rameses lay nearby, reduced to a
dilapidated state with mostly a few courses of stone
remaining. Daniel's gaze went further afield to the ruins
of a mud brick temple in the northwest, an old kingdom
temple dedicated to Khentiamentiu.

The sight of it, and the conjuring up of the name
Khentiamentiu, brought back Daniel's old hunger to
explore that he so often subdued these days.

"Do you mind if I leave you and the lawyer to keep an
eye on the fractious family for a while?" he whispered to
Kate. "The guide will take you on to the Osirieon next, a
mysterious sunken temple built out of megaliths with
water and an island down below. They used to think of
it as another tomb of Osiris,. I'm going to slip away and

ask our driver to take me on a spin across the plain to look around."

"Enjoy," she said. "I'm loving this tour and just stretching my legs."

Their Land Cruiser followed the direction of the ancient processional *wadi* that led to the tombs of the first Dynasty pharaohs, including that of King Djer, the symbolic tomb of Osiris.

The plain also held Ibis and dog cemeteries in honour of the death dogs of Abydos.

"Where are you, Khentiamentiu?'" Daniel murmured to himself.

They bounded in the four-wheel drive vehicle over the desert terrain while he studied it through the windscreen and passenger window.

Rubber-on-the-ground archaeology, he thought, as they crossed the ancient plain of the afterlife.

The man-god Khentiamentiu, represented by a jack-dog, bore a title. "Lord of the Westerners.' Westerners, referring not to a cardinal point, but to the direction of the setting sun, the land of the dead.

"Maybe we'll go closer to the mountain cliffs," he suggested.

The driver changed course.

The decision almost catapulted them into the land of the dead, when a rip of gunfire smacked into the side of their vehicle.

The driver scowled in his rear view mirror.

"Bad. Maybe looter gang."

"What do they want with us?"

"Not me. Their bullets are all on your side. Do you have something they want?"

"Only my skin, apparently."

"I saw men follow your group into the temple from the car park," the driver now informed him.

"Okay, maybe it's time to cut this excursion short. Can you get us away from these lunatics and back to the temple?"

"Hold tight, Sir."

The driver swung in a sharp circle and hit the accelerator, surging towards their pursuers. A risky move because as they approached on a collision course, an attacker leaned out of a window and took another shot that blew away Daniel's side mirror.

"I said get us *away* from them."

But the driver had a plan.

He spun the Land Cruiser at the last moment, just as they hit a soft bank of sand. The swerving vehicle threw a broadside of sand into the windscreen of the oncoming attackers, blinding them.

The man-made sandstorm prevented them from seeing a hidden outcrop of rock. They hit it on the driver's side and it threw the vehicle over.

Looking back, Daniel saw it spinning on its back like a stranded tortoise.

The sand of Abydos could be a weapon as well as hide secrets.

Who were they?

Calder Hall's deadly murder mystery game was over.

Why try to kill him?

He rejoined the group as they were returning to the car park outside Abydos temple.

"No dramas in the temple?" he said.

"None, but you look a bit shaken about," Kate said. "No dramas on your desert drive?"

He wanted to say no, but the truth took over his tongue.

"Oh, you know, a mad car chase and then gunfire from a band of antiquities looters, that sort of thing."

"Sure, Daniel."

In the afternoon they sailed on to Nag Hammadi, where the *Belle Epoque* moored for the night.
The mood on board had lifted a little after the Abydos excursion and they brightened even more over cocktails at sundown, followed by bottles of wine over dinner. The sisters closed ranks with Big Brother and shared a table with him at dinner. Daniel and Kate sat at a table nearby and the lawyer dined alone at another. Uncle Bryan also preferred his own company.
The dinner and the night that followed were uneventful.
But not the morning.

Legal Suit marched in with the sober air of a lawyer serving a legal document, the young Egyptian camera girl following in his footsteps.
"There's been another death overnight."
Big Brother.
No signs of anything suspicious.
"He died in his sleep, it appears."
"The Sisters?" Daniel said.
"Distraught," Legal Suit said.
He didn't need to ask about ex-cop Uncle Bryan.
He'd be exploding.
Even if he was the guilty party. Maybe more so.
But he remained an unlikely candidate in Daniel's view.
The Sisters would be his first choice.
But why would they take such a spectacular risk?
Only... if they were absolutely certain that their involvement would never be proved.

Daniel met the ship's doctor in the boat's surgery.
The young filmmaker Mayet was there too, recording it all, camera in hand.

If this continues, the old man could have a ring of
subsidiary burials, Daniel thought grimly.
The doctor drew the sheet off the bulking form on the
bed.
"A big man, it could have been a heart attack," he said.
"Not poisoning?"
The doctor dropped his voice to a confidential murmur.
"By poisoning I take it you don't mean food poisoning.
There is no sign of say arsenic poisoning, which leaves
bluish discolouration in the mouth area. More likely it
was a brain aneurysm, a silent killer that can strike
anyone at any time.
A remarkable convenient occurrence, Daniel thought.
Time for a chat with the sisters.

He visited them in their cabin. They let him in and
retreated to a couch where they resumed their knitting
with neurotic intensity. Maybe they planned to yarn
bomb the boat.
Mayet recorded the discussion.
"When did you last see your big brother?" he said.
Click, click, click...
The sound of deathwatch beetles.
"We had an after-dinner drink in the bar and then
separated. We came back to our cabin."
"We know what it must look like –"
" – and we know what you must be thinking –"
" – that you are the last ones with any motive to harm
your brother." Now he was finishing their sentences.
"Your Uncle Bryan has never been in the running."
"Maybe."
"But we didn't do anything."
Maybe, like Isis and Nephthys, they were spinning a
shroud for their brother's body.

Daniel inspected Big Brother's cabin. The bed was still rumpled, everything left as it was.
No sign of violence.
His shoulders slumped.
What would a detective do now? Go over the details again. Repeat an examination of the facts.
What would an archaeologist do?
Dig new exploratory trenches? In which direction? Try some ground penetrating radar to look below the surface?

Belle Epoque continued on the next leg of the cruise and arrived at Qena at mid morning.
A tour to the temple of Dendera was in the offing and it was a temptation, but out of the question after recent events. And yet the temple of Dendera was one of Daniel's favourites, dedicated to the goddess Hathor.
He had always admired the double-headed columns inside the temple with capitals showing twin images of a cow-eared woman.
The Female Soul With Two Faces.
Like the Sisterhood, he thought.
Stony.
But right now he desperately needed to see below the surface.
Below the surface?
Time to repeat an investigation of the evidence.

Uncle Bryan interrupted him on his way. The ex-cop came boiling up the stairs and grabbed Daniel by his shirt. He shoved Daniel against a curved wooden railing, tilting him off his feet.
'Excessive use of force' was probably a valid charge against him after all, Daniel thought, and there was excessive strength in the grizzled man's grip. Daniel

wondered if he needed to kick himself free with a well-aimed knee.

"Listen, archaeology man, you're screwing up and I've had enough. Another death and you haven't even interviewed me."

Daniel tried to keep calm.

"You sound disappointed. You angling to be guilty?"

"I could be guilty of hurting you right now with one push."

"Don't."

"What happened to my nephew Leo?"

"Enquiries are proceeding –"

"– don't give me that police statement bullshit."

' – and progress is expected soon."

Uncle Bryan relaxed his grip and Daniel sank back to the step.

"That better be true."

Stone Hathor, Female Soul with Two Faces

Legal Suit and Mayet, the voyage filmmaker, joined him at a second meeting with the sisters in their cabin.

"We told you everything," the sisters said.

"Everything? A classic case of pulling the wool over my eyes. I underestimated you two. Your late Big Brother warned me that you have clever fingers, but you're also manipulative. I imagined you weren't even listening to my lectures as you sat there with your balls of yarn and flying knitting needles. But you listened all too closely. You knew you weren't going to win a massive inheritance by knitting."

"Or listening to lectures on ancient history."

"Ancient history was all our father cared about. Not us."

"Do you know what the boat's doctor found when he examined your brother in his surgery? Nothing. Not a mark. Like the 'unblemished beast sacrifices' of animals. Or those murdered servants and subjects of early pharaohs that I talked about in my lecture, their practices of so-called 'retainer sacrifices' and 'subsidiary burials'. I conjectured about how the victims might have been killed. Strangulation? Poison? Or maybe by means of a sharp instrument penetrating the brain, say from under a raised eyelid, where it left no mutilation, not even blood. Especially if somebody used a sharp instrument for the murder - like a fine knitting needle."

The sisters gave up knitting at precisely the same moment.

'Now only their foreheads are knitting in displeased frowns,' he thought.

"Here's how it happened," he said. "You encouraged your brother to get rolling drunk at dinner and afterwards, probably helping him back to his cabin, where he passed out on his bed. Then you took one of your finest knitting needles, flipped an eyelid up and goodbye Big Brother and your rival for a fortune. The trace of a puncture to the brain was almost invisible, but after my suspicions, and a second examination by the doctor using a magnifying glass, he found it. I'm

sure a proper autopsy will confirm it. Quite subtle,
Ladies."
"And our father thought we were stupid –"
"– and never remembered anything about ancient
history."
"You will remain confined to your cabin, behind a locked
door until the end of the cruise at Aswan," Legal Suit
said.
"We're prisoners?"
"You'll have your meals and refreshments brought to
you."
"And you'll have all the time in the world to knit," Daniel
said. "Especially after your trial."

VIDEOCAM CAPTURES DANIEL LEAVING THE CABIN.
(Young female voice, off camera):

"You must be pleased with that stroke of inspiration. No
detective would have solved that. It took specialized
historical knowledge."

**"Thank you, but I'm left with the awful thought that
my lecture gave the sisters their idea. They had no
interest in ancient history, their father said. So I
excited their interest and fed them a piece of arcane
historical conjecture that got the eldest brother
killed. And I thought knitting was a gentle pastime!
It must have taken nerve on their part, and greed, to
go through with it."**

Well played, Daniel," Kate said later. "The sisters were
doing it for themselves,"
"Yes. And so well co-ordinated they could have knitted
together with one set of needles, like two hands playing
chopsticks on a piano."
"But did you ever notice what they were knitting?"

"No."
"Scarves. Yards and yards of them," she said.
"Like mummy windings. Those two always made me think of Isis and Nephthys, weaving what were called the 'tresses of Nephthys' for the body of the dead Osiris. That only leaves Uncle Bad Cop now. But I'm sure he doesn't stand a chance of scoring the inheritance."
"Then I wonder what happens now? Who inherits?"
"Probably archaeology. Some university institution."
"Then why play games?" she said.
Ironic, coming from Kate, he thought.
"You mean he should have just given it to archaeology straight away and saved all this violence? Calder was a successful movie producer, remember. They're no strangers to violence. And he hated his family as much as they hated him. He also wanted one last bit show."
"Sad."
"Murder, I'm discovering, is a sad business. Sadder than archaeology, digging up the past..."

Karnak Temple

CHAPTER 10
"Tell us the truth!"

While Daniel appreciated the funerary beliefs of the ancient Egyptians, a funerary barque was not his idea of a cruise.

Now there were two bodies on board.

As well as two killers in detention.

The *Belle Epoque* churned onwards to Luxor, amid growing cruise boat traffic that clotted the artery of the Nile. They berthed at the busy tourist hub, with the backdrop of the Winter Palace Hotel facade and the columns of Luxor Temple dominating the town.

Luxor - once famed as *'Thebes of a Thousand Gates'*. Now a thousand entry gates, Daniel reflected. Ticketed entryways to great temples like Karnak and Luxor, Medinet Habu, Deir el Bahari, tombs in the Valleys of the Kings, Valley of the Queens and nobles, the Western Valley, the fine Luxor Museum and more...

He needed this escape.

Daniel, Kate, Mayet and the lawyer took a break from the boat to make the tour. Uncle Bryan stayed on board. First stop was a trip by vehicle across a Nile bridge to explore the Valley of the Kings and Hatshepsut's temple. It was Kate's first visit and the carved and painted underworlds of the tombs beneath the valley, deep and glowing, enthralled her with every step.

For Daniel, the tombs this time were like a sense of failure closing in, especially the small dimensions of Tutankhamun's tomb.

Luxor and particularly Karnak temple, with its acres of stone and crushingly huge hypostyle columns added a weight to his spirit.

Could he have done more to anticipate disasters?

'He's certainly put me in one,' Daniel thought.

It should all be over, but there was something unfinished about this Murder on the Nile Mystery Cruise.

He needed time alone to think.

He left Kate and Legal Suit with the Egyptian guide to complete their tour of Karnak's adjoining open-air museum and strolled out to the car park.

The temple was a lot emptier than he remembered on past visits and the car park was the same, with fewer coaches, minibuses and cars in evidence.

Maybe he'd take a rest in the air-conditioned vehicle and wait for the others to come.

The driver would be waiting, probably smoking a cigarette outside.

Daniel circled a blue coach. It had curtained off windows.

They weren't curtains to keep out the sun.

Three men jumped him and before he could struggle hauled him on board the bus.

It wasn't over.

The three Egyptians, in western clothes, worked him over inside the cigarette smoke fug of the bus and the fourth one left the driver's seat to help.

Blows rained on Daniel like the rotating paddles of the riverboat that had clubbed the body of Calder Hall.

He was groggy and his head spinning when they flung him down into a front seat.

"Search him."

Fingers dug into pockets, hard hands frisked him.

"Is that what you wanted to do to me at Abydos, when you tried to shoot me? Hoping you'd find something on me? What?"

"Nothing on him," the searcher said.

Then the interrogation began.

"You tell us the truth. How long do you know rich man Calder Hall?"

"I only met him only once before."

That got him a slap.

"The truth."

"Once."

"Another slap across the cheek.

"How long?"

"Only once before and when he hired me…"

Another slap. The truth could be painful. What did they want him to say? Lie and say that he was a lifelong confidant? They'd prefer a lie evidently, but he couldn't get his tongue to say it.

"He knew a secret about Abydos, but he was dying," the Egyptian inquisitor said. "Dying with his secret. Then he calls on you. Why?"

"I don't know why. I wish he hadn't."

A ripping backhand across the other cheek now. Daniel's head rang.

"Why did he hire you? What did he say when he first hired you? What did you talk about?"

"Dogs, walking sticks, Abydos…"

"Aha, Abydos. What did the rich man know about Abydos?"

More truth was probably going to get Daniel another slap.

"He liked the place. We both had a special interest in it."

"And your special interest?"

"Just a wild theory about lost tombs still to be found in Abydos."

"Did he know about such a tomb? Did he ask you to join him in finding it? What is in this tomb?"

"Maybe the treasures of Khufu?"
The Khufu theory had always been a stretch for Daniel,
a hypothetical teaser, and sounded much more so now.
"Khufu?" The interrogator slapped Daniel harder. "You
think we are stupid? That is the biggest lie of all. The
Great Pyramid was Khufu's tomb."
"Yes, but..."
Crack.
This blow went across the head.
He couldn't help letting out a loud groan.
"Tell us the truth!"
Daniel blinked up at them blearily.
"Okay, your coach door had just opened and two armed
tourist police are coming in here."
"Lies!" But the interrogator turned to look and so did the
others.
It was not some lame trick to divert them so that he
could turn the tables and fight his way out.
Two policemen, rifles pointing, were there.
Somebody must have seen the attack and reported it.
"Step out of the bus. All of you!"

The doctor aboard the *Belle Epoque* checked out Daniel
on his return.
He'd survive, with a few painkillers to ease the aches
and pains.
"So you really were shot and chased back at Abydos,"
Kate said.
"I told you the truth."
"You made it sound like a lie."
"It just sounded unbelievable. Like that attack at
Karnak."
"What is happening, Daniel? Something is going on
besides this Nile murder nightmare."
"Calder Hall liked putting people in challenging
situations. I just don't know which one he's put me in
now."

That night the sisters committed joint suicide in their cabin.
Tablet overdoses, the doctor said.
Why hadn't Daniel anticipated the danger?
Uncle Bryan wondered too.
"We've had two murders, one escape, and two suicides on your watch, Buddy. That adds up to one big balls-up!"
Hardly a successful investigation, Daniel supposed, even though he did pick the killers.
"Well, don't take things too hard," he soothed the ex-detective. "Hey, you're the last man standing. But at least you're innocent, well not of everything. You've never been a suspect here. And never a prospect to inherit. In fact, I've been wondering why you're here at all. And I think I've worked it out. Your brother liked putting people in spots. He knew a detective would make things tough for me and provide an entertaining contrast to an Egyptologist at work and that's the only reason he invited you along."

The last two stops of Edfu and Kom Ombo went by in a blur of painful memories and puzzlement for Daniel.
Everybody stayed on board.
Then they arrived at Aswan, a rural town in Egypt's far south.
They berthed opposite caramel cliffs with sweeping stairs that climbed to reach the Tombs of the Nobles.
The end of the Nile murder mystery cruise felt like an anticlimax.

Aswan tombs

CHAPTER 11
A Will to astonish

But it wasn't quite over.

There was still the remaining part of the Will to address, which Legal Suit insisted on doing in a corner of the public lounge aboard the *Belle Epoque,* joined by the official recorder Mayet, behind her camera, and Uncle Bryan seething in his chair.

Daniel was surprised to see the lawyer rest the old man's walking stick against a coffee table.

The stick rocked and the golden jackal-dog shook his head.

"What else is there to learn?" Daniel said. "I suppose Calder Hall's fortune is going to Big Archaeology - some overseas university with missions in Egypt?"

"No. One of my deceased client's relatives survived the cruise."

Daniel blinked in surprise.

"You mean Uncle Bryan, here?"

"No, I'm afraid. Sorry," he said to the ex-policeman who grunted.

"Why am I not surprised?"

"Then the young ship jumper, Computer Guy? He's been found?"

"No. He will be found and arrested, be assured, but not him, either. Someone else will inherit the fortune. Someone who remained hidden throughout the cruise."

That took a moment to sink in.

"A stowaway?" Daniel said.

"Not exactly. She is watching us right now - from behind that camera."

"Mayet?"

Daniel swung to the camera.

All he could see of her head was the front of the camera and her beret poking out on top.

"I can now disclose that producer Calder Hall's young filmmaker protégé is in fact his unrecognized daughter to an Egyptian woman twenty five years ago. But now the daughter is recognized, and handsomely so!"

Mayet, the unseen one, hidden behind the camera all the time. The silent observer, like an invisible narrator of a drama, her recorded images running like a stream, or river of consciousness through a journey of over half a thousand miles.

Calder Hall had set her secretly among her undeserving siblings for a telling, side-by-side comparison. It suddenly made the father's threat of only ONE beneficiary a little more understandable.

Mayet was the sole heir.

Calder was launching the young Egyptian into a career of big filmmaking with a fortune at her disposal.

Daniel had never seen that coming.

He too had looked for some tiny redeeming feature in the legitimate family members. If one of them had a glimmer of virtue in spite of their criminality, it had been Computer Man. During the family's discussion after the bombshell announcement, he had made the suggestion that whoever inherited should forgo their rights and share equally with the others. He had also shared some of his ill-gotten gains from hacking in the past with his ungrateful sisters.

"Did any of the other family members come close?" Daniel asked the lawyer.

"I am not at liberty to speak about that. But now that the cruise is over, you will of course be paid the full balance for your services."

"Thank you. Well there it is. I suppose we'll now call in the Egyptian authorities to try to clean up this mess."

"Yes. But first there was a small bequest for you, a gift, a memorial of Mr Hall, if you like. He wanted you to

have this." He picked up the golden-headed walking
stick and handed it to Daniel.

"He's giving me the stick? Hello, Jack," Daniel said to
the jackal-dog, clasping the stick in his hand to address
the canine head.

"My former client also left this message for you."
The lawyer read out a note:

*"Daniel, here is a gift for you. The Opener of Ways.
Here's hoping he can help you open the ways to your
dream discovery.*
*I like giving people challenges... and I'm leaving you with
one."*

"Please thank the Estate of Calder Hall for me," Daniel
said. "Maybe with my luck I'll break a leg next and really
need this guy." He turned to the camera. "You can come
out now, Mayet. Time for the hidden filmmaker to take a
bow. Congratulations on your sensational inheritance!"
The camera trembled.
Mayet came out now, smiling, dampness on her cheeks.

"Lucky Mayet," Kate said afterwards in their cabin.
"Funny if she had been the murderer all along, while
hiding behind the camera."
"Please Kate, no more. I'm over murder mystery games."
"But it's possible, you know. Think about it. She would
have had access to the old man's computer too. She told
us the old man watched updates of her footage at the
end of each day. How would that happen? She'd
download footage to his laptop for him to view at his
leisure. Maybe he trusted her and turned his back and
she saw something on his computer. Thought she had a
chance of inheriting something, but the old man was
dithering in his deliberations and so she had to stop
him making a change."
"Oh, God," he said.

Had he been wrong all along?

"But why would Computer Guy jump off the boat in such a guilty way?" he said. "If Mayet was the guilty one?"

"Maybe they were both guilty. Maybe they had discovered each other's secret prying into the old man's computer diary notes and decided to act together."

"Oh God," he said again.

"The look on your face. I'm only teasing. I don't believe Mayet is like that at all. She is a lovely Egyptian girl. Trust my instincts."

Kate was always going to be playful and games were going continue he thought.

"Oh, good," he said, but it made him a little fearful about how close he might have come to the brink of disaster as an archaeologist detective.

"And yet..." she said.

"Stop it."

They packed to leave the boat.

Legal Suit had booked them into Aswan's Old Cataract Hotel overlooking the rock-strewn Nile, the last stop on their itinerary, where they would stay as the official investigations proceeded.

CHAPTER 12
Opener of Ways

Daniel and Kate were relaxing on the Old Cataract balcony that overlooked the Nile. Down below, tilting sails of feluccas cut the blue water like white diamonds as they glided past.

The Egyptian police had swarmed over the *Belle Epoque*, statements had been taken, followed by polite, but tireless questioning. The missing son had been picked up by authorities and would be duly charged.

"This grand hotel, perched on a cliff above the Nile, is where Agatha Christie wrote her detective novel *Death on the Nile*," he told Kate over a beer on the hotel balcony. "I wonder what she would have made of our little murder mystery game?"

"Not enough bodies or red herrings for her."

"Quite enough."

"That stick suits you, you know Daniel," she said, eyeing the jackal-dog walking stick resting on the table edge between them. "Gives you an Edwardian air. Gentlemen sported sticks in those days, didn't they?"

"Jack and I are just bonding. I think he's hoping we're going to provide his new 'forever home'."

"Forever? We?"

He nodded, picked up the jackal-dog's head stick and made the canine nod too. She laughed and patted its head.

The Opener of Ways.

There seemed to have been a loaded significance in Calder Hall's last message to him, the thought kept teasing him.

The old man had left him with the *Opener of Ways*. *"Here is a gift for you. The Opener of Ways. Here's hoping he can help you open the ways to your dream discovery. I like giving people challenges... and I'm leaving you with this one."*

"Hang on," he said.

"Changed your mind already?"

"Maybe I need to do a little more digging, with Jack."

"Jack? What do you mean?"

Daniel grasped the head of the walking stick and gave it a twist.

"Why are you strangling him?"

The jackal-dog resisted. Daniel's hand trembled with the
force he applied, then, like a jammed tap handle
suddenly giving way, the dog twisted his head.
"There."
Now the golden head spun as Daniel unscrewed the
walking stick's handle.
"What are you looking for? One of those old fashioned
swords in a cane?"
"No. But something equally pointed."
She sat up.
"What?"
The head came off to reveal an empty tube.
He peered down it. Not quite empty. A rolled up cylinder
of paper lay coiled inside.
He shook it out, put the jackal-head and stick on the
table and unfurled the paper.
"It's some kind of map?" she said, excited.
"Correct."
He squinted at the drawing. It showed an embayed plain
with mountains, temples, cemeteries marked on the
surface.
One of these, a dog cemetery, had been ringed in red ink
with a single word beside it.
'Khentiamentiu!'
The *eureka!* name.
But not a lost tomb, it was only a dog cemetery.
Unless... there was a hidden tomb below it in the depths
of Abydos sand.
Was that why it had remained hidden from archaeology?
Not even ground penetrating radar had seen it because
it was disguised by the structures of the dog cemetery
above it?
Dead dogs, concealing the death dog Lord of the
Westerners.
"What is it, Daniel?"
"The key. Calder Hall has given it to me. And the biggest
challenge of all. To spend my future trying to convince
Big Egyptology to listen."

**"So now I have the truth.
And the truth is that Calder Hall's game continues
with a different challenge of detection - an
archaeological one. How did he come by the
knowledge he has passed on to me? He had many
contacts in legitimate Egyptology and it would be
surprising if he didn't also have a few on the shady
side too.
It could be that this story is still the beginning and
the issue of Calder Hall's legacy to his family was
merely a violent backdrop to a more astounding
legacy - a secret that he knew I would never give up
on.
Modern Egypt has suffered instability, a revolution,
wholesale looting, a crisis of tourism worsened by a
pandemic that has spurred illicit digging and
trafficking. Maybe somebody came across something
and owed Calder a favour, so they shared a secret
discovery with him. A secret others would
desperately want to know. I may never find out the
answer.
It remains to be seen if, after bringing archaeology
to mystery murder detection, I can now bring
detective skills to archaeology and uncover the
truth about Khentiamentiu."**

Daniel checked the surface of his tongue in a bathroom
mirror of the Old Aswan Hotel.
Had the mark faded a little? It was still discernible.
'What if it's there for good?' he thought.

Ancient Egyptians believed that magic was about unseen, hidden connectedness between things, words, ideas, dreams, truth, reality, symbols…
Maybe he was stuck with something.
A marked man.
He'd played a role of investigating crimes with the mark of Maat upon him, finding truth, weighing the guilt and innocence of others in the balance.
Was he fated go on playing the role of an archaeologist detective?

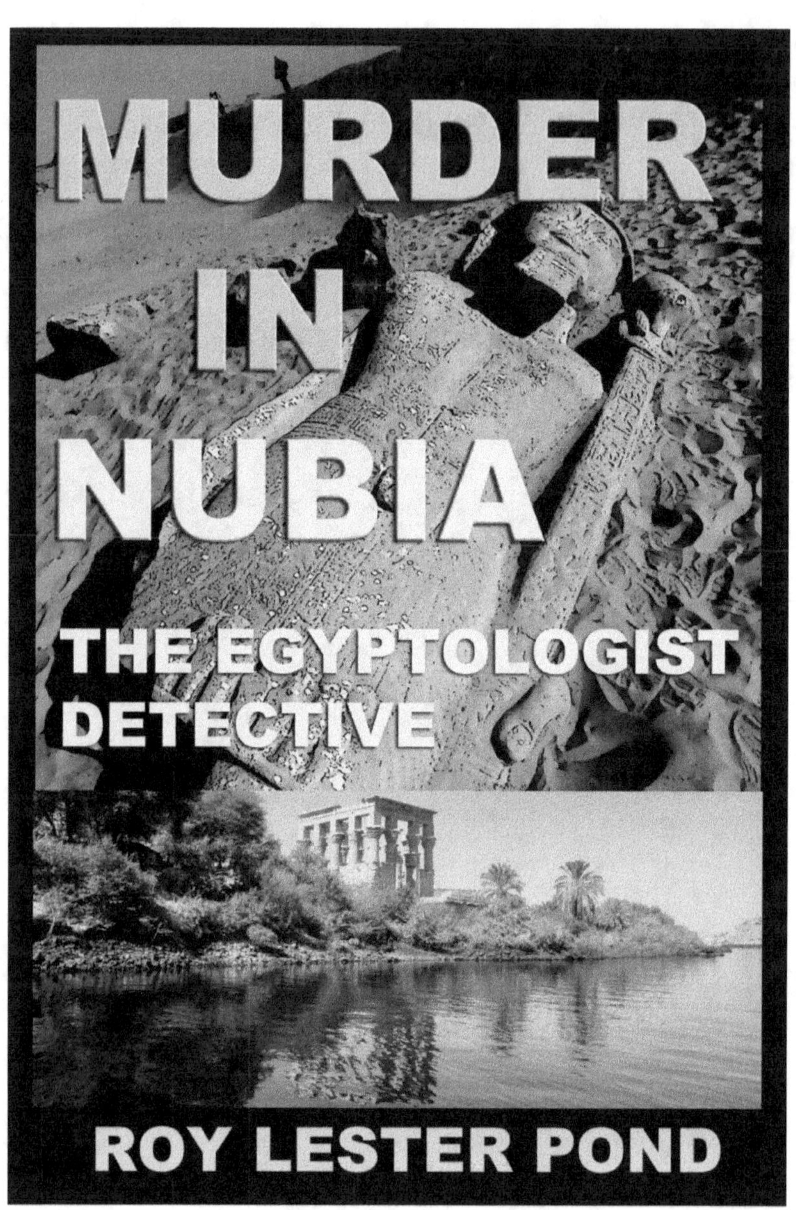

MURDER
IN
NUBIA
THE EGYPTOLOGIST
DETECTIVE
ROY LESTER POND

CONTENTS

CHAPTER 1
Life in ruins

Daniel Cane sat waiting in the Departure Lounge of Cairo Airport, his girlfriend Kate beside him, when it hit him.

The lustre of his chosen career of Egyptian archaeology, pursuing a boyhood passion, had faded.

Archaeology was tone deaf today.

Maybe even stone deaf.

Daniel felt the weight of truth land on his shoulders. Digging up the ancient dead in their tombs was enthralling, yes, but behind the times, like a dusty old paperback copy of Ernest Hemingway's *Death in the Afternoon*, glamourizing bullfighters in Spain, or *The Snows of Kilimanjaro*, glamourizing big game hunters in Africa.

It was an old joke, but perhaps an ironic one, that 'an archaeologist's career lies in ruins'.

Right then, his did. Or so it felt to him.

And it was the saddest moment of his life.

"What's wrong, Daniel?" Kate said. "You're pouting, but not in your contemplating way. More like a sulk. You ought to be relieved. We're finally getting away."

That was true.

Away from Egyptian officialdom.

The civilization of ancient Egypt had stretched for aeons and modern Egypt's criminal investigation process was not far behind, he'd discovered. The Egyptian authorities had only recently wrapped up a prolonged police investigation and court proceedings into the Murder on the Nile Mystery Cruise affair, and Daniel and Kate were about to leave after an extended stay.

"Just thinking," he said. "Were heroes of archaeology like Howard Carter and his sponsor Lord Carnarvon little better than big game hunters - hunting the biggest game of all? The golden glory of a buried pharaoh. Then displaying the finds like sporting trophies."

"You're taking a dark view of archaeology these days. What's come over you?"

The truth, he thought, glancing at the necklace around Kate's neck, a golden chain suspending a green faience image of the goddess Maat, ancient Egypt's goddess of Truth, a neat, squatting lady with a feather of truth on her head.

He had given it to her as a gift after a visit to the *Khan al Khalili* bazaar in Cairo.

It reminded him of a moment during their recent cruise on the Nile aboard the luxury vintage paddle wheeler, the *S.S. Nile Epoque.*

He'd been brushing his teeth one morning in the cabin's marble and brass bathroom when he'd spotted something odd on his tongue.

A blemish on the surface. Coffee stain? No, not a stain, he decided, diving close to the mirror again. An image. A green feather shape. Painted on the surface of his tongue in outline.

A feather?

"Wha- tha- hell?" he'd said around his protruding tongue, like a victim of strangulation, his eyes splashes of wonderment.

He wiggled the tongue. The feather shape danced.

Some unknown Nile contagion? Maybe fur on his tongue after drinking old-fashioned gin slings with Kate the night before?

No, a distinct feather shape, drawn in what looked like green ink.

He spat out. He gargled with water. He brushed again. Rotating-oscillating bristles on the head of his electric toothbrush tickled the buds of his tongue, but failed to remove the blemish.

Then he recalled that in ancient Egypt the symbol of an ostrich plume represented the goddess of Truth, Balance and Justice, Maat. Priests of the Goddess of Truth drew a small image of the feather of truth on their tongues with green dye so that the words they spoke would be the truth...
One of Kate's little games, he'd surmised.
After drinks the night before, he may have been snoring with his mouth open, and Kate had playfully sketched the symbol on his tongue using green eye-liner.
That was so like Kate.
He'd thought of accusing her, but the symbolism of the mark on his tongue struck him with the force of a revelation. It was as if he'd awoken with a mysterious gift from the dream world and he was afraid of talking it away.
Maybe I'll just hold my tongue for now, he'd thought.
The mark had faded somewhat after the cruise, but was still there. Stubbornly.
Was he going to bear the mark of truth forever?
"Archaeology is destruction, a fact widely recognized," he said, his voice a murmur in the airport's Departure Lounge. "Archaeologists destroys context irretrievably, every time they dig up a tomb. But we also destroy something else. The sacred."
"So you have a down on all archaeology. You'd rather Nefertiti's bust remained lost under the sands, instead of becoming an icon of art that enriches the world?"

Her unadulterated enthusiasm for everything ancient Egypt was a balm on his disillusionment, but little more.

"No, I'd dig up Nefertiti's sculpture a hundred times over," he admitted truthfully. "Her painted bust in the Neues Museum is like a lovely ancient sunrise. But it doesn't quite let my profession off the hook and the German archaeologists who dug her up didn't find her in a tomb, but inside a sculptor's studio."

"I am sorry to interrupt your travel plans at this advanced stage," an Egyptian man in a suit said to them. "I am Ahmed Khadir, Supreme Council of Antiquities."

Daniel silently groaned.

Egyptian officialdom had pursued them to the Departure Lounge of Cairo Airport.

"They're about to announce our departure," Daniel said in protest.

"You have been cancelled," the man said.

"Our flight cancelled?"

"Your tickets. Forgive us."

The official did not come alone. He'd brought along a pair of tourist policemen, and his smile did not succeed in warming up the cold steel of their machineguns or the draught of officialdom he brought with him.

"Oh Daniel, no," Kate murmured. "I thought the case was finally over."

"Not the case," the Egyptian man in a suit said, overhearing her. The Egyptian official reminded Daniel of the pharaoh Senusert III, depicted in statues with radar-dish sized ears, suggesting that the king 'heard all', even the whispers of his subjects.

Officialdom. Polite, but unwavering. It was here again.

"I meant it is not about the case that I have come here at this last critical moment," the man said.

"You wanted to say an official thank you and goodbye, and maybe just make sure we left?" Daniel said.

"Not the case, either. We must detain you."

Detain?
Detention in Egypt was ominous.
"There is a private meeting room here at the airport. We ask you both to join us. Please, come this way."
Daniel rose reluctantly. 'I should never, ever have involved myself in criminal investigation', he thought, a sentiment he'd fingered over and over again like beads on a rosary during the painful and painstaking investigations following the Nile Cruise business.
What now?
The tourist policemen, weapons slung over their shoulders, wrangled their two bags of hand luggage. Daniel and Kate followed the Egyptian official out of the Departure Lounge, just as the loudspeaker crackled. *"This is the first announcement for the departure of flight..."*
So close to escape.

It may have looked like a last-moment interception, but the Egyptian official had evidently made preparations. He had a PowerPoint presentation lined up on a laptop on a meeting table in a private room and invited them to sit facing a screen.
The official clicked a button.
A colourful image of the island Temple of Philae at Aswan in Egypt's south brightened the meeting room. Written against the temple backdrop were the words:

"The Great Return to Egypt"

THE GREAT RETURN

It had the feel of a tourism promotional campaign.
'Have we been strong-armed into a market research interview?' Daniel wondered.
He hadn't noticed any clipboards in evidence, although there were a couple of Egyptian officials sitting at the table with notebooks, one a woman wearing a headscarf. The antiquities official addressed his captive audience.
"To mark the return of tourism and international interest in Egypt's antiquities, following political and pandemic uncertainties, a gala reunion and Congress of the world's Egyptological community and ancient Egypt lovers is about to take place, not in Cairo, but far south at Aswan's Philae Temple. *The Great Return to Egypt.* Historically, the Philae Island Temple was the last ancient Egyptian temple practicing the old religion until closed down by orders of the Roman Emperor Justinian. Here, the last priestly-scribe chiseled the last ever hieroglyph in the stone, before ancient Egypt's religion, the old gods and the old written sacred language, fell silent. What better place for a great return to Egypt?"
"It's a favourite temple of mine," Daniel said. "But why not use the new Grand Museum at Saqqara as a draw card?"
"That has its own Cairo-centric energy and focus, along with the Great Pyramid and the Sphinx. We need to stretch the world's focus of interest to all of Egypt, in particular to treasures that are less celebrated, such as Aswan and Abu Simbel in the far South."
"Yes, I heard something was in the planning. Good luck with the event, but I'm puzzled about why we're getting a preview."
"We want you to be there at the event."
Daniel blinked at him in surprise.
"This is a strange way to deliver an invitation," he said, thinking of the armed guards who now waited outside the meeting room door. "An email would have done."
"We wish to hire you to attend, not as a delegate, but as an undercover investigator."

"Listen, I am not –"
Khadir held up a hand.
"– and before you say you are not a policeman or a detective, but an archaeologist, let me remind you about your impressive detective work on the Nile cruise murders that I have heard all about."
"One role and I'm typecast."
"We need somebody inside the tent of international archaeology at this event as well as our own Egyptian security."
"What do you think is going to happen?" Daniel said.
"We have heard things," and here the official tugged at a pharaonic ear lobe. "Hidden warnings of harm against international keynote delegates. Death threats. Perhaps not everybody welcomes a great return of the ancient past and may plan to harm those at the event. This is a new beginning for Egypt on the world stage and it is too important to allow any unfortunate incidents to occur that may further delay a great recovery."
Somebody wants to kill the key archaeologists of the world?
Interesting, and almost understandable, Daniel thought.
"But who do you suspect is behind it? Islamic extremists?"
"That is one possibility. There are others. We have made a list."
Khadir pressed a button and revealed a drawn-up list of suspects on the screen, which he read out.

- Radical Islamists hostile to a renewed focus on ancient Egypt's pagan history

- Fundamental religious extremists from the west. They do not welcome the return of Egypt's 'evil' magic and pantheistic influence. Ancient Egypt represents the carnality and idolatry of the world, according to the Christian Bible

- Neo-paganists and occult organisations, who work for a New Age world order and the return of the old religion and have a grudge against academic denigrators of mythology

They had done their homework.
Daniel pursued his lips thoughtfully, a habit in contemplation.
"You overlook two other groups with a motive for disliking archaeology," he said.
"We are all ears."
"Cultural activists - those who hate the western world's museums and the Egyptological establishment because of their refusal to return Egypt's antiquities."
"Ah yes. The repatriation zealots."
"On steroids. And finally, the gods themselves."
"The gods?"
"Philae Island Temple was the final exit point of the gods before they were forced to leave their realm on earth," Daniel said. "As you said. The Great Return to Egypt! What a perfect setting, and time, for some ungodly revenge on archaeologists who have desecrated their holy sites."
Daniel was kidding, but Khadir's eyes widened and Daniel was sure the great ears flapped.
"We need a fertile mind like yours, Daniel! I will be there in an official antiquities capacity and will be keeping my ear to the ground. But you and your good lady can mix freely among the guests."
Mix?
Daniel was a loner who'd secretly embraced the era of social distancing. A solidly-built, outdoorsy man with a preference for the solitude of the field, or of the library, crowds suffocated him more than the closed spaces of passages and tombs.
"I was asked as an archaeologist to play the role of detective on my last cruise, in a mock-murder mystery game that turned deadly real. Now you are asking me to

play secret agent, or at least undercover investigator. Maybe I need an acting agent."

"We must penetrate any conspiracy and prevent incidents."

"Why not cancel the whole event?"

"Too late now and we would lose face, as well as demonstrate a lack of confidence in the renewed Egypt that we seek to project to the world."

"Fine, but I'm a bit weary of playing roles," Daniel said.

"Ah, but are you weary of playing the archaeologist?"

How could he possibly know?

"What do you mean?"

"We have an offer for you. We know you have theories about a lost site in Egypt's Abydos area. Help us now and we will look at progressing your ideas later."

The SCA on his side.

It would mean ultimate access and support.

It would be better than teaming up with an international university mission, if that were even possible. The SCA could cut red tape for him and put him in the box seat to pursue his theories about Abydos and the tomb of Khentiamentiu, and he'd have a team of talented Egyptian archaeologists at his disposal. This was a once in a lifetime opportunity for an outsider like him.

But now?

With his enthusiasm for archaeology lying in ruins?

His qualms about archaeology were being tested, he guessed.

Go after sullied glory or be content to be a regular cruise Egyptologist for the rest of his life.

How damned ironic.

"Do I have your ear?" Khadir said. "Once again you will be joining a cruise as a guest Egyptologist. Not a Nile cruise this time, but a cruise across the inland sea of Lake Nasser in the desert of Egyptian Nubia. It will be a welcoming lead-up event and also a reunion for a celebrated archaeology team that made the amazing discovery of the Golden Seth Tomb near Kom Ombo,

which as you know, is also in our far south, just fifty kilometres from Aswan. To draw attention to our neglected Southern treasures, our gala cruise will sail from Abu Simbel in Egyptian Nubia to Aswan before the open air marquee congress at Philae.”
“The marquee where you want me to be inside the tent?”
“Quite so.”
Khadir flashed up a scene of a cruise boat on Lake Nasser in front of the temple of Abu Simbel, with the colossi of Rameses the Great providing a grand, but stony reception.

Abu Simbel Temple in Egypt's far south

121

Khadir continued.

"A luxury cruise of several days that will precede a world congress on the jewel of Philae Island, home of the temple of Isis."

Khadir flashed up views of the temple complex on the screen. "Here on the night of the first session with all still present, there will be a grand opera festival with singing, dancing and boats on the lake. It is based on the very, very great Festival of the 'Return of the Wandering Goddess', a mythological story that culminated each year at Philae."

"I like the idea," Daniel said, "the tale of the goddess who deserted Egypt in a huff, leaving Egypt vulnerable without her divine protection, and wandered off into Nubia, where she had to be tricked and tempted step by step into coming back, by the baboon god Thoth."

Khadir laughed.

"Warning! Spoiler alert! You have given away the story to your lady friend here."

"Sounds intriguing," Kate said.

"What is your answer, Daniel?" Khadir pressed him.

"There will be a generous fee for you and, of course, all expenses will be covered for both you and your lady companion."

Philae Island Temple complex

CHAPTER 2

Abu Simbel Sound and Fury

"Well?" Kate prodded Daniel. "I'd like to see Abu Simbel
and cruise Lake Nasser - and this is a chance to pursue
your Abydos theory afterwards. Just the opportunity
you've dreamed of."
"Me snooping around with a bunch of archaeologists on
a cruise?" Daniel said. "That's not a role I fancy
somehow."
"They are not all archaeologists," Khadir said. "With
seventy cabins on the cruise boat, there will be well over
a hundred passengers on board. Ancient Egypt
aficionados, celebrities, journalists, even a famous
writer of murder mysteries. Many other attendees,
however, will be skipping the cruise and going straight
to the Philae Congress later."
"A famous writer on board? Which one?" Kate asked.
"Jemma Karnak, a pseudonym I believe."
"Jemma Karnak! I devour her books!" Kate said,
clapping her hands. "She writes brilliant Egypt-based
crime mysteries. Oh, Daniel, I'd love to meet her."
Daniel was not a particular fan of crime fiction, but like
most people on the planet he'd heard of Jemma Karnak.
The lady had once been a groundbreaking archaeologist
herself - in every sense - before turning away from
trowels and brushes to the business of creating
sensational, best-selling fiction.
He saw Kate's imploring look.

She had suffered the tedium and stress of the
investigation and the trial at his side and deserved some
recovery time.

He looked at Khadir.

"You're asking me to act as the cruise Egyptologist on a
boat crammed with Egyptologists?"

"Your onboard lectures will not be designed for them.
Your talks will inform and excite the laymen."

"I know Egyptologists. They'll be there for the blood
sport, critical knives sharpened."

Khadir waved away his concerns.

"You have cruised Lake Nasser in the past, Daniel, and
given on-board lectures, I understand. Simply recycle
your material, while bearing in mind our new theme of
'The Great Return to Egypt.'"

Pressure?

What pressure?

They took a flight from Cairo to Abu Simbel, along with
the Egyptian SCA lady dressed in a headscarf. Her
name was Randa and she would be his facilitator and
link with the SCA.

"Mister Khadir will be joining us at Abu Simbel before
the cruise," Randa told them.

"It's a mountain of pharaohs!" Kate said, looking up at
the colossi of Rameses the Great in front of the Temple
of Abu Simbel, three of the statues intact and the fourth
toppled from the waist after an early earthquake.

"Yes, a mountain moved by UNESCO and the Egyptian
government, sixty-five metres higher up, and two
hundred metres further inland, to rescue it from
drowning in the rising waters of the Aswan Dam. I
thought I'd give you a quick preview of the place before
boarding our boat. Don't forget we're coming back this

afternoon for a welcoming get-together, and a 'Sound-and-Light' Show after dusk."

Cruise boat berthed near Abu Simbel Temple

The cruise boat cleaners snapped on new rubber gloves. Cleaning and disinfecting protocols after the Covid-19 outbreak were going to die hard. Not least here on a cruise boat berthed at Abu Simbel on Lake Nasser in the far reaches of Egypt.
The housekeeping crew was in.
A pair of them laboured in a bright, roomy cabin with picture windows looking out onto the calm waters of the inland ocean.
The man and the woman operated like a surgical team, anonymous in masks and gloves. The man, a Nubian, wiped and sterilised surfaces clinically with disinfectant, while the Egyptian housekeeping maid refreshed the linen, changing the bedding to crisp new Egyptian cotton sheets. One corner of the top sheet bore a logo crest of the cruise boat, a graphic that looked a bit like a clinging beetle. Or worse.
It suggested something else today and the hair on the maid's arms reacted as if it had touched her skin.
"Are they gathered outside yet?" she said to the Nubian in Arabic. "Check and see."
She meant the passengers who customarily wheeled up their luggage to the stone wharf and waited for clearance before boarding. In the wake of a viral pandemic, cruising today called for a greater measure of patience on the part of passengers and crew.
He gave a grunt and stepped outside onto the teak-boarded deck to check.
The housekeeping maid was alone at last.
Time to do it now, follow the secret instructions she'd been paid handsomely to complete.

She looked down at the perfectly made bed. Tightly drawn hospital corners and the top sheet crisply folded back at a regulation sixteen centimetres. Then in a fluid motion, she destroyed her perfection, ripping the fold back with one hand while sweeping a glass flask from her bosom.

She gave a twist of her scarfed head to check on the door.

Quick.

She flipped open the lid of the flask and tipped the contents between the sheets. Fat, wriggling black question marks, barbed hooks with metallic legs spilled out, untangled themselves and scuttled apart, dramatic living graphics against pure whiteness. Desert scorpions - displayed against a background of one-thousand thread Egyptian cotton.

A final shake and a strip of paper fell out between them. Printed words on its surface said:

Tomb Robber, may the scorpions' stings be against you and your greed, and strike with the fire of the god's anger

The housekeeping maid snapped the folded sheet back over the squirming, waving barbs and clamped the sides tightly, sealing it like a lid. She would add the weight of the pillows and bed cover to keep the creatures inside.

"We must hurry," her Nubian cabin cleaner said, returning. "With these social distancing rules still hanging over us, the queue of passengers almost stretches back to the Temple!"

"I am near the end," she said.

So was somebody else's life near the end, she thought with a shiver.

A cluster of hooks awaited them in their sleep tonight, venomous hooks amid soft bedding.

It was a perfect trap.

Alluring and yet deadly at its heart.

The attendees in front of Abu Simbel looked like an adoring throng of subjects at a triumphal royal appearance, a royal impact quadrupled by multiple stone colossi.

Social distancing rules had spread out the attendees at this celebratory event. The guests lined the stone forecourt like a crowd of royal watchers and in fact most eyes drifted up to the overpowering cliff-kings on their thrones.

The official speech by the Minister of State for Antiquities seemed to resound in honour of Rameses. Over a speaker system, the voice of the Minister rang out with phrases such as 'The Great Return to Egypt...the Mother of History. Here we stand before the statues of mighty Rameses the Great, as Egypt begins a triumphal new era for tourism and for exciting new discoveries", but he might just as well have been trumpeting paeans of praise to Rameses the Great:

"Rameses, Beloved of Amun, Ra has fashioned him, The strong bull... Rich in years, great in victories..."

Daniel smiled to himself as he recalled spotting a carved relief of Rameses on a wall within the dimness of the temple and pointing it out to Kate. It showed Rameses worshiping *himself*, burning incense before an image of himself as a god.

Rameses clearly wasn't the last demagogic character to display such self-reverence, Daniel thought. Today, psychiatrists would diagnose it as *narcissistic* personality disorder.

In keeping with the new protocols, guests were handed individual canapé trays, each with a convenient slot for a cocktail glass. Neat, and safe, but holding their trays gave guests the air of waiters.

Randa, the dutiful Muslim in her attractive headscarf, who had joined Daniel and Kate, stuck to mineral water, he noted. He had taken to her, a strong, dignified and pleasant woman.

He decided to call on her knowledge.

"Do you see any likely suspects, or targets, around, Randa," he murmured, casting a sweeping glance over the assembly.

"Targets? Randa said. "I suppose any of the Egyptologists here, like that famous group over there, an archaeology team. The discoverers of the golden Seth tomb at Kom Ombo. That striking man with the beard and the white suit is Professor Harvardson, joint field director of the excavation. And the lady beside him in the designer gown is his new Egyptologist wife Nadine..." The young woman had an expensive look to her and she leaned into his side. A new wife, no doubt, he thought. Much younger. "That tall man nearby is a bio-archaeologist, then another senior archaeologist, and beside him an epigraphic expert, not that they found much in the way of inscriptions in their sensational tomb discovery. On the edge is the Egyptian co-director of the dig, Abdul."

It was evident that old ties overcame social distancing, Daniel observed. The archaeologists stood noticeably closer than other attendees, except perhaps for the Egyptian.

"Never mind archaeologists," Kate said, excitedly. "I spot Jemma Karnak over there - and the best-selling author looks exactly like her photos on her book covers."

If she did, it was no accident, Daniel thought. The crime author was a carefully curated woman, who combined an ancient Egyptian appearance of bobbed dark hair and arched painted eyes with a vintage art-deco style dress that had the simplicity of style of ancient Egypt.

"I know Jemma quite well," Randa said. "Shall I ask her over?"

"Not necessary –" Daniel began.

"– oh yes, please do, Randa. Before somebody else latches onto her," Kate said.

"She is clever and well-connected and could be a useful ally for you, Daniel."

Daniel shrugged.

He must wrestle down his natural social-distancing reflex, he thought, a handicap for a man hired to play the role of investigator.

As Randa brought her over and made the introductions, he felt the stare of Jemma Karnak's painted eyes under the arched Nefertiti eyebrows.

"So, Daniel Cane, our cruise Egyptologist," Jemma Karnak said. "I must say you're a brave man to give lectures with the cream of Egyptology on board."

The voice, like her face, was beautiful, but sharply faceted. Maybe the pressures of success and fame had hardened her beauty like pressure hardened a diamond, he thought, noticing the rock on her hand. Not a ring on the engagement finger, he noted. Nor a marriage ring.

"Brave may not be quite the word," he said.

"Perhaps not," she said. "Strange, might be better. I heard about your celebrated role as a detective in the mock-murder cruise affair and I'm wondering why you'd jump straight into another cruise. And also," she said throwing a smile at their Egyptian companion, "why you are so friendly with our Antiquities officials, even though Randa is a darling lady. Are we expecting more trouble, another murder or two?"

Jemma Karnak was sharp in every respect.

A crime writer, he reminded himself.

"Are you trying to make me give away a plot?" he answered in a non-committal way, though unable to lie.

"Jemma's plots are brilliant," Kate enthused. "I have read nearly all of her books. Are you here researching material for a new mystery to write, Jemma?"

"No, I'm not writing this time, I'm just living it, taking advantage of this great reunion occasion to re-visit some of my favourite places."

Daniel was curious about her background.

"I understand you were a pioneer in the field of archaeology before you turned crime author," he said.

"Yes, just as you are an archaeologist turned detective."

"Then you know all the players here?"

"What do you want to know?"

"About that clique of archaeologists over there."

"The Dream Team. I was part of the dream once. The Field Director Professor David Harvardson and I were a team of another kind. Married, you see. You wouldn't know it, but I was the one who first proposed the existence of a Golden Seth tomb and where it might be located. We worked together near Kom Ombo, on the Wadi Hammamat gold route to the Eastern desert. Kom Ombo was the god Seth's sacred nome, called *Nebt* by the ancient Egyptians, meaning "City of Gold." I was proved right, but sadly, I did not get to prove it for myself." She sighed over her glass of champagne, clouding the glass briefly like the shadow that passed over her expression. "But that was a long time ago, and today I live a lavish lifestyle that no archaeologist digging up sand could afford. This is the first time I've even been in the company of the team since we broke up."

Somebody else soon latched onto Jemma Karnak. A journalist broke in and swept the famous author away for an interview.

"And what about suspects?" Daniel said to the Supreme Council of Antiquities woman.

"Those with a hate on Egyptology, who might like to harm the Great Return to Egypt?" Randa said. "Muslim extremists? It's possible some Egyptians here, or crewmembers on the boat, could harbor secret resentment. Western religious fundamentalists? There is a rich sponsor of Bible-based archaeology here... Who knows?" She frowned. "Perhaps we should fear some occult, New Age crazy person..."

"Careful, Randa, Kate is New Age."

"A bit. But not all crystals and stuff," Kate said.

"And hardly hostile to Egyptology if she is your lady friend, Daniel," the Egyptian woman observed with a smile.

"I suppose not. Kate's more earnest about ancient Egypt than I am these days."

This investigation was not going to be easy, Daniel thought. And the cruise was only the first part of it. A congress on the mysterious island of Philae with its nest of temples awaited them afterwards.

Later, the guests wandered in small, spaced groups through the inner temple of Abu Simbel, the hall flanked by standing, Osiride-style figures or Rameses, the walls alive with images of the ubiquitous Rameses offering sacrifices, smiting enemies, winning battles, swinging a mace and drawing a bow in his speeding chariot.

"Why build all this spectacle out here in the desert of Nubia?" Kate said.

"It's more than just a canvas for Rameses and his boasting about dubious military victories, such as the Battle of Qadesh against the Hittites. This temple in the furthest reaches of Egypt is like a remote missile base," Daniel said. "It stands as a psychological and esoteric threat. The scale of the emplacement is meant to strike awe and fear in the Nubians in the South and the sympathetic magic carved on its walls, the smiting and crushing of adversaries, Nubians, Hittites, Syrians, is designed to inflict long range magical destruction on enemies as well as stave off the forces of chaos."

Daniel wondered privately: 'Can I stave off the forces of chaos threatening this Great Return to Egypt?'

Was a killer among them walking inside the temple? Maybe that bulky man admiring Rameses as the king launched arrows at the enemy? Or that nun-like figure of a woman in a hijab headdress, looking up at the brandished club of Rameses?

As darkness fell, the guests gathered outside for the Abu Simbel Sound-and-Light Show. In deference to the new protocols, the organizers had dispensed with headphones normally used by guests to hear commentaries in a range of languages. Instead, a single English narrator told the story of the temple in Shakespearean tones, along with the music and laser-and-light dazzle of the show projected onto the surfaces of the Rameses temple and the adjoining temple of Queen Nefertari.
He wondered if Rameses, intermittently illuminated by the spectacle of dazzling beams, would have been dismayed to see the golden-face of Nefertari projected in gigantic size, drowning his statues like the waters of the lake.

The tall archaeologist, a member of the Dream Team, shed his clothes on a cabin chair by the light of a bedside lamp and, dressed only in boxer shorts, stretched his long frame towards the ceiling one last time before bed.
His joints cracked and he sighed at the pleasurable prospect of rest and sleep.
The cabin's double bed looked as inviting as a pool after a hot day in the desert of the south and a whispering air-conditioning vent above cooled the space.
He couldn't wait to slide himself between those crisp white Egyptian cotton sheets and stretch out his tired limbs.
All that standing around outside the temple, all that small talk, all that electronic sound and fury and laser light wizardry had drained him.
He pulled away the folded and tucked-in sheet corner to release it.
Tight, crisp, reassuring, like hermetic sealing.
Virginal.

He slipped in a toe, then his foot, ankle and leg. Smooth
and cool.
He felt his skin crinkle with pleasure. Then with a little
jump, like a swimmer breaking through the coldness of
water in a pool, he invaded the purity of the bedding
with his entire body.
Because he was a tall man he reached to the end and he
stretched out his legs and arms to relish the coolness.
With his neck and head in the pillows, his body made
an Egyptian five-pointed star like the ones painted on
the ceilings of tombs.
But the pain that followed was like a crucifixion.
Soft pillows muffled his cries

Cruise boat berthed at Abu Simbel

CHAPTER 3
Cruise into murder

It was Daniel's first lecture as the official cruise Egyptologist, convened after morning tea and Egyptian pastries, in a vintage lounge area furnished with cushioned chairs and couches, spaced out and arranged in a semi circle.

As he guessed, the Egyptologists were present, front and centre, the whole Dream Team, except perhaps for the tall archaeologist who was missing. Maybe he'd slept in or was lounging somewhere in the back.

Professor Harvardson and his clingy wife sat in front, with an air of faintly amused expectation.

Ignore them.

There was a good turnout of other passengers to concentrate on in the spacious area, including the crime author Jemma Karnak, who sat next to Kate and the Supreme Council of Antiquities people.

"Welcome to this floating diorama of salvaged history. During our cruise stops along the shores of Lake Nasser," Daniel began, "your Egyptian licensed guides will be showing you around the temples of Nubia, rescued from the rising water of the dam, so I won't be covering that now. Except for a few relevant photos." Daniel clicked a button and images appeared on a screen.

RESCUE ARCHAEOLOGY SAVED THIS
SAVED THIS

SAVED THIS
BUT WHAT
CAN SAVE ARCHAEOLOGY
TODAY?

"Archaeology and Egyptology are approaching something of an existential crisis today. Here in the 'woke' era, we keep on waking up legions of the dead from their centuries of sleep under the flashing eyes of press cameras. Recently they dug up a cache of sixty coffins in Saqqara and lined up the dead under a tent with the press taking photos, looking like a display of pandemic mortalities. But it was more like Covid-19 in reverse, because here they were bringing up dead bodies to the surface instead of putting them down under the ground.

Sadly today, it's Egyptology and archaeology that are in danger of drowning in a new tide of modern sensibility..."

That unsettled the Dream Team.

The young wife slid a hand around Professor Harvardson's arm and the man gave an agitated rub of his short beard before speaking out:-

"Excuse me, but before you commence your presentation – "

"– I've already commenced."

"Are you speaking to us as an archaeologist who has ever found anything in the field that advances the science?"

"Ah, science. The white-coat word that is meant to cover up a multitude of sins... but does it? Are we advancing science or sensationalism?"

He'd rattled the Dream Team, but the passengers were sitting up with interest. There was nothing like a fight to get a crowd around you, Daniel thought.

"You'd rather Tutankhamun's golden mask remained lost under the rubble of the Valley of the Kings?" the young wife asked.

"Now we jump from science to art. And gold! What about excessive exhumation of the ancient dead? If something gives us a twinge of unease today, it will horrify us tomorrow. Like the sharp division between Egypt's cultivated greenery and the parched sand of the desert,

we need to find a line that avoids disrespect and
sensationalism and this collectors' mania that makes us
look like hoarders of the past. The great return to
Egypt? How about a simple return to seemliness?"

"That was brave," the author Jemma Karnak
commented afterwards, as the passengers drifted out of
the Lounge.
"You mean calling out archaeology's sins in front of the
Dream Team?"
"No, in front of the SCA. Those were Egyptian
archaeologists digging up that cache of mummy coffins
in Saqqara, good men working as respectfully as they
could. Aren't you biting the hand that feeds you?"
"It's their future I'm trying to protect too. What are your
feelings about wholesale archaeology today - as
someone who is a bit of an outsider yourself these
days?"
"I hate to agree with my ex-husband David on anything,
but I wonder if you'd have said all that if you had found
a great intact tomb."
"Maybe I'll never find out."
"Don't mind Daniel," Kate said to her. "He's a bit dark
about archaeology these days."

They gathered in the archaeologist's cabin like a team of
doctors around a hospital patient's bed.
But the patient beneath their gaze was dead.
"Scorpions?" Khadir said, tugging at a pendulous
earlobe.
"Scorpions cannot get in here," the Egyptian Boat
Manager said. "It is impossible."
It was late morning and the dead archaeologist had
been missing for a number of hours.
The boat had sailed and stopped alongside the island
site of *Kasr Ibrim,* a ruined citadel rescued from lower

Nubia, not open to visitors, and most people had skipped the viewing from the sundeck, in particular the Egyptologists on board.
Nobody had missed the archaeologist until later.
He had been stung to death by scorpions in his bed.
Victim to the strikes of lashing tails.
Daniel felt imaginary scorpions tickling up his spine and gave a shiver.
"Multiple envenomations," the cruise doctor said. "It induced coronary arrest. He died last night."
"Clearly introduced," Daniel said. "Where are they now?"
"They?"
"The arachnids."
"Safely gathered up in a jar," the Boat Manager said.
"How many?"
"Does it matter?" Ahmed Khadir, the SCA official, said.
"It might."
"They found seven scorpions."
"Are you sure?" Daniel said.
"Housekeeping scoured the cabin. Two of the scorpions had been crushed in the bed. Perhaps the victim's beating and thrashing around might have made matters worse, attracting more attacks."
"Intriguing."
"Horrifying is a more fitting description," Khadir said.
"No, I mean the significance of the number. Seven. You see, Isis had a train of seven scorpions. They followed her in her wanderings, according to mythology. And our cruise is heading, where? Philae, the temple of Isis."
"As an official in antiquities, I regard Egyptian mythology as respectfully as any, Daniel, but you're not suggesting –"
"– I'm suggesting it's no accident. But I suppose murder never is."
Khadir frowned.
"Somebody wanted to reference the gods of Egypt?"
"The printed note would confirm it."
Daniel read it out:

***Tomb Robber, may the scorpion's stings be against
you and your greed, and strike with the fire of the
god's anger***

"It's also couched in the style of a curse against tomb
invaders, invoking the vengeance of the gods," Daniel
added.

"A killer who violently opposes the work of Egyptian
archaeology," Khadir said. "It is as we feared. A
disaster."

"Especially for this man, a star Egyptologist."

"Yes, of course, but also a disaster for our Great Return
to Egypt initiative."

"Then we sail back to Abu Simbel?"

"By no means. That would create a stir. Besides, the
facilities at Abu Simbel are limited. Better that we
continue as normal to Aswan. We have a cold room for
the remains."

"What will you say about this to the passengers - to the
man's close team of colleagues?"

"What do you suggest?"

"We must tell the truth, of course. He succumbed to
scorpion venom."

"Perhaps not so unexpected," Khadir said. "The temple
of Abu Simbel lies in the desert and scorpions are
always a presence in the open. And then there was the
darkness of the Sound-and-Light Show..."

"But multiple scorpions?"

"We do not need to go into too many details," the Boat
Manager said anxiously. "I would prefer also that there
be no mention of multiple scorpions inside one of our
cruise boat cabins. It would cause unnecessary panic
among the guests."

Khadir nodded.

"Discretion, of course. And we should hold back details
of the note at this stage. People don't have to know
everything at this time. A full investigation will take

place and matters will be resolved in Aswan, we may tell them."

True. But of course, the initial investigations could not wait and would begin immediately.

Khadir took Daniel aside on a deserted stretch of deck overlooking the jagged ruins of *Kasr Ibrahm.* The site looked to Daniel like decaying molars sticking up out of the rocky jaw of the island.

"We must work fast, Daniel. This may only be the start. Who do you suppose could have acted against this poor man?"

"Who planted the crawling assassins?" Daniel shrugged. "Maybe the archaeologist carelessly left his cabin door open for a while to grab a breath of fresh air on deck. Then the killer slipped in unnoticed and deposited them inside the bed. Maybe staff did it, while delivering something. Or housekeeping may have been involved. Those who cleaned and disinfected the cabin and made up the bed."

"Naturally, the Boat Manager will identify the cleaning staff who last serviced the cabin and they will be taken aside for questioning. Do you wish to be present?"

"No. I'm not sure I could pick out a lie in Arabic, anyway," Daniel said, surprising him. "Let the Boat Manager go ahead. Besides, if some staff members were involved, they'd only be acting as tools, employed by someone else. Acting for remuneration, or out of duress."

"But –" Khadir said.

"This is not the act of disgruntled hospitality staff. You said yourself there had been warnings of harm against international keynote delegates. I don't see cleaners and housekeepers formulating such a plot. It's more sophisticated than that. And whoever wrote that threatening note understands the pattern of protective tomb curses. But if the Manager has any suspicions after an interrogation, then please let me know immediately."

“So where do you begin, Daniel?”
“We can’t be sure of the archaeologist’s enemies, but we do know his friends. I need to interview the Dream Team.”
“The celebrity archaeologists who discovered the golden Seth tomb at Kom Ombo?”
“Exactly.”
“You will need to interview them one at a time, I expect.”
“No, that doesn’t work for me, certainly not at this stage. I prefer to see the way they react among each other, watch the group dynamics. Often more revealing, I find.”
“You are an unusual detective.”
“That’s because I’m an archaeologist. We dig for stuff, yes, but we draw conclusions by analyzing context as well as the objects themselves, stratification layers, position, relationships and so on. Contextual archaeology. An object out of context, might as well be sitting apart in a glass case without a label of provenance.”
It sounded plausible, but Daniel was hoping that an approach he had taken in the past would work for him once again.
Sometimes you had to put people together and shake them before they’d rattle.
He doubted they’d be helpful in answering his questions after his recent presentation about the status of archaeology in the modern age.

Kasr Ibrim, ruins of an island citadel

CHAPTER 4
Death on the Nubian sea

Here they were.

Every academic's nightmare, gathered in a comfortable lounge with the doors locked.

The peer group.

The bearded archaeology team leader Professor David Harvardson and his young Egyptologist wife Nadine sat on a couch together.

The others sat in spaced out chairs, the Egyptian co-director, another senior archaeologist, and also an epigraphic expert who had a chair closest to Nadine. The group looked as stony as the seated statues of Rameses II left behind at Abu Simbel Temple as they faced Daniel and the two Supreme Council of Antiquities members, Ahmed Khalid and Randa who had come along for official support.

Professor Harvardson went on the offensive to set the terms of the discussion.

"Before you trot out the official line that this was some accident, we've already figured out that it isn't."

"How is that?" Daniel said.

"It's unusual for adults to die from scorpion stings, though he did have a heart condition. But if Doug had been stung that badly at the Sound-and-Light Show, he would never have made it back to his cabin and we'd certainly have heard about it. He was sitting nearby us throughout the show and not even the dramatic music and narration would have drowned out his agony. Scorpions don't nest together, anyway. They hide individually under rocks. Somebody must have tipped a bucket of the creatures over him when he got back to the boat."

"Who do you think might have wanted to harm him?"
Daniel said.
The professor's eyes glinted in reply.
"I am prepared to accept that under SCA auspices you
are playing the investigator here and I am willing to
assist the investigation, but I am not willing to do your
job for you."
"You must have some ideas."
"Whereas you - maybe not," the Professor said.
"But I am curious. You - maybe not," Daniel said. "Don't
you have any theories about your colleague, as the dead
man's expedition leader? Or is it a case of one less
member in the Dream Team meaning more golden glory
to share around?"
The Professor jerked up his head.
"That is offensive."
"Maybe you are not a person who has theories. Even
about tombs."
"I see. You're trying to provoke me, using this
opportunity to attack a real world, successful
archaeologist and not a cruise guide. Here's a theory for
you. It's a waste of time talking to us. You need to be
out looking for real suspects."
"Do you feel threatened as archaeologists?" Daniel said.
"Not in the way you suggested in your presentation. But
threats against those opening tombs are commonplace.
Archaeologists are used to seeing them. The team that
found Tutankhamun received threats and warnings,
Howard Carter, Lord Carnarvon..."
"Have you received threats?"
"We all have. Not unexpected with such a widely
publicized find."
"Speaking of the find... who found it?" Daniel said.
"We did."
"No dispute about that?"
"Oh, the usual local presence in Egyptian archaeology
tried to lay claims. But fortunately we had an SCA

approved Egyptian Egyptologist co-director in Abdul
here, so there was no room to muscle in."
"What about a prior team member? Jemma Karnak, the
author. You were once partners in every sense. For what
it's worth, she says the theory of the missing tomb and
its location was originally her idea."
"She would," the new wife Nadine snapped, as if she
were the wronged woman in the relationship and not a
young marriage wrecker. "Nothing can take the credit
away from David..."
Here the other team members stirred.
... and from the team," she added.
"The thing about my ex-wife Jemma that you should
know, is that she makes up lies for a living," the
Professor said. "She writes fiction and she has a fertile,
not to mention lucrative, imagination. She struck gold
after our parting," he said with a resentful flash, "while I
have to live on the modest rewards of a university
tenure. I did her a favour. Anyway, that all happened
years back and we haven't seen each other since.
Jemma has never attacked us. Not a word in years. And
Jemma hates scorpions and crawlies of any kind.
Anyway, why attack Doug? If she still resents anyone it
would be me - or Nadine. This is a tragic business and
clearly deserves more professional investigation."

He found Kate stretched out on the sundeck engrossed
in a novel.
"Jemma Karnak's latest murder mystery - and this copy
is signed by the author herself."
Kate held up the fat paperback, revealing a front page
covered with a mannish scrawl like a jagged
cardiograph.
"It's too much to hope it's a written and signed
confession from Jemma," Daniel said.
"Not of any crime, but it is a confession of sorts. I'll read
it to you.

Maybe Jemma Karnak was growing a little ambivalent about archaeology too, Daniel wondered, though a light he'd detected in the author's eye suggested the passion still burnt there.

"How did your meeting with the team go?" Kate said.

"Not exactly a dream, I'm afraid. I've got that drowning feeling as if the lake out there is over my head."

He gazed out morosely at the waters of Lake Nasser that gave way to empty desert beyond. A lifeless shore with scabs of black rock protruding like volcanic eruptions in the heat. This lake stretched for half a thousand kilometres with an average width of twelve kilometres and a depth that could swallow the highest temple.

It could be a Martian landscape out there, Daniel thought, if water like this existed on Mars, and he might as well be on another planet now, feeling surprisingly alien among fellow Egyptologists.

"A *deben* for your thoughts," the author Jemma Karnak broke into his reflection, referring to the ancient Egyptian monetary measure. "The classic scene of the detective mulling over a case."

"He pouts when he does it," Kate said. "But your detectives never do that in your books."

"No, they wallow in their cogitation, like hippos in the mud. That's the time when they feel most alive. May I join you?" Without waiting for an answer, she slipped onto a recliner beside Kate. "I still love to watch someone reading one of my books and I've been known to linger opposite a reader in a cafe or airport lounge, that sort of thing, hidden behind my dark glasses. Writers never get over that pleasure. They're touchingly grateful that someone is giving life to their characters and plots in their minds as they read, because that's what readers do. Books are just dead trees without them. And speaking of plots, we have a real life murder on our hands. Don't raise your eyebrows at 'murder', Daniel. Word is buzzing around the cruise boat already. How perfect for you - and for me!"

"You don't sound devastated about the loss of a former colleague."

"Douglas was pretty shabby with me. They all were, which surprised me. You'd think we'd had a team divorce and they all took the separation as a personal affront. I can understand David shutting me out after the divorce, but I never expected the others to close ranks like that. But returning to the crime. Our cruise boat has sprung leaks, you see. Rumours trickling out. I've heard whispers that the scene of the crime was a nest of scorpions." She gave a shudder.

"Scorpions don't nest, I'm told," he said.

With her crime author's ear to the ground, Jemma Karnak had gleaned the truth.

He couldn't lie. He watched her face as he said: 'one thing struck me as significant. The number of scorpions involved. Seven. Isis had seven scorpions that followed her."

"A mythological echo," Jemma said, impressed. "That's pretty clever. Maybe you should be writing crime fiction."

"Playing detective is enough of a stretch. Playing crime writer... well, I'll leave that to you."

"I understand there was a note involved."

"You are well informed." He recalled the words of the murder note once again: 'Tomb Robber, may the scorpion's stings be against you and your greed, and strike with the fire of the god's anger.'

Written by somebody familiar with protective tomb curses and smiting texts and who knew the pattern of them.

"Somebody who has a grudge against archaeologists, evidently," Jemma said.

"And I wonder who might have a grudge against archaeologists?" Daniel said distantly. "Someone abandoned by one, and kept out of a discovery they might have shared?"

"Congratulations. That makes me Suspect Number One. Of course, you know that it's a canon of detective crime fiction that it's never the first suspect who's found guilty at the end. No, I'm afraid you're going to have to dig a bit deeper. But I'm tickled to play the villain for once."

"Jemma has very kindly given me this copy of her book as a gift, Daniel," Kate said reprovingly. "I hope you are just teasing her."

"No, he's not entirely, but I'm really not offended. It's like a reward for someone who writes about dastardly murder plots all the time to be thrown into one herself. You've won me over, Daniel, and I'm happy to play your female, literary Doctor Watson, and help you in any way I can. As long as I don't place my own neck in an Egyptian hangman's noose, of course. Do you suppose modern Egyptians use *halfa* grass for rope making as the ancients did? Hate the thought of that prickly fibre!"

Grim joke.

But Jemma was a murder writer.

The Egyptian SCA official Khadir appeared, ears flapping.

"Sorry to interrupt. Daniel, a moment. Excuse me, Ladies," he said.

He took Daniel aside.

"The Boat Captain has interviewed the cleaning staff. They stand by each other and say they refreshed the cabin together, working as a close team. Sorry, no answers there. How are you progressing? Did I happen to overhear you accuse one of the world's most famous writers of being a suspect?"

Those Pharaoh Senusert ears heard everything that the people whispered.

"Not in so many words."
The official gave a grunt.
"I am relieved. Jemma Karnak is a one-woman
promotions unit for Egyptian tourism. Her writing has
attracted more people to Egypt than Agatha Christie's
Death on the Nile."
"It's Death on the Nubian Lake that concerns me now."
"What about your interrogation of the archaeology
team?" Khadir said. "Have you drawn any conclusions?"
"Plenty, but I'm not sure where they point. Remember
that list of disaffected groups we discussed at the
airport meeting. Radical Islamists hostile to a renewed
focus on ancient Egypt's pagan history, Fundamental
biblical extremists from the west who see Egypt as
mammon, neo-paganists with a beef against
Egyptologists, and the cultural repatriation activists..."
"Not forgetting the wrathful gods of Egypt," Khalid said,
straight-faced. So he had got the joke.
"My point is, can you point me to any guests who might
represent those points of view, even though they might
be masking their hostility?" Daniel said.
"There is a neo-pagan leader of a spiritual organization
on board, a Lady who styles herself as an Egyptian
priestess of Kemet, Kemet of course being the ancient
name for Egypt. Several of these organizations have
sprung up in the West."
"Yes, but in my experience they encourage discovery -
they want to learn more about ancient Egypt's religious
practices so they can adopt them," Daniel said.
"Next, there is a rich Biblical archaeology sponsor who
has stated that he deplores bringing glory to ancient
Egypt and only sees its value as support for the Bible.
He believes that Egypt is the last stronghold of Egypt's
demonic gods who still want to spread their evil and
control the world. Crazy?" He shrugged.
"And zealots of cultural repatriation?" Daniel said.
"Activists who want Nefertiti's bust back from Berlin

and The Rosetta Stone Back from London... for starters."
Khadir gave a wry smile.
"They may hide it. But every Egyptian on this boat longs for that, my Friend, especially me. But please don't make me a murder suspect too."
"Maybe let's start with the sponsor of Biblical archaeology."

Lake Nasser, a desert Martian landscape

"Do you have a problem with archaeology in Egypt?"
Daniel asked.
 The billionaire sponsor of an American university's
Biblical archaeology mission shrugged.
"If I do, then I've mistakenly spent a lot of bucks doing
it."
"But Egypt is merely a backdrop to you, a religious
backdrop to Biblical revelation."
The middle-aged man rolled his eyes behind his golden
glasses
"That's where so many are people today are being fooled.
Egypt is not a backdrop. The world is still under
bondage to the gods of the Egyptians, just as the book
of Exodus showed the Hebrews to be under bondage to
the gods of the Egyptians. I'm not the only believer to
claim that the Covid-19 pandemic was a demonic force
let loose from ancient Egypt. A curse from a hidden,
demonic stronghold of Egypt's gods in existence today.
Whatever triggered it was not a wet market in China's
Wuhan province. Something mysterious is at work. And
I believe it started in Egypt. Egypt represents the world
and the home of spiritual idolatry. Egypt is the symbol
of this world, not to mention its obsession with the next.
Ancient Egypt - most forcibly in scripture - is Exhibit A
for vainglorious power, riches, mystery, magic, demonic
forces, alluring temptation, sensuality, death and
resurrection as well monumental *hubris* on the scale of
the pyramids. 'Exodus' stands as the epitome of struggle
against 'evil', as represented in the Bible by Egypt...
*'On all the gods of Egypt I will execute judgments: I am
the Lord.'*
*'But they rebelled against me and were not willing to
listen to me. None of them cast away the detestable
things their eyes feasted on, nor did they forsake the
idols of Egypt. "Then I said I would pour out my wrath
upon them and spend my anger against them in the
midst of the land of Egypt.'* And even then, the fleeing

Israelites in the desert continued to lust after the 'fleshpots of Egypt'."

"So you might not approve of ancient Egypt becoming a renewed focus in the world," Daniel said. "Or of archaeologists who help make it so."

"Do those archaeologists know what they have opened up? Seth was the Egyptian name for the demonic force we call the devil. They have let death and destruction into the world by opening the tomb. The devil's tomb."

"And they deserve death for that?"

"That is for a higher power to decide."

The Book of Two Ways - underworld map painted on a coffin floor

Digsite at Wadi Hammamat, beyond Kom Ombo,
a few years earlier.

It was an intact tomb, though un-inscribed, choked with gold, and the news and images of rich treasures had been flashed around the world.

But unlike the dreamy gaze of a boy king like Tutankhamun, the discoverers had been met with ominous statues and a death mask formed into the shape of a golden head of a snarling creature, the mythical Seth-creature thought to have had the hooked snout of an okapi or a donkey.

The ancient cedar coffin lid of the tomb owner had long since crumbled away and the rest of the cedar base had deteriorated into cubicle-like segments, like eroded rift canyons or the scales of a crocodile.

The female Egyptologist Nadine touched one piece with a brush and it crumbled away like cigarette ash under the lightest pressure.

What was left of the mummy, a shell of congealed dust, had already been gingerly removed and taken away to a storage magazine, but a piece of adhered linen shroud left behind still obscured the coffin's floor.

"We don't need a scanning electron microscopy to show that there's been catastrophic microbiological attack here," the bio-archaeologist said looking into the wooden ruins.

"As well as extreme age."

"Wood borer at the head and foot."

"It's not a coffin. It's a heap of powder. No gap filler can save this."

"Let's try to peel off the section of linen and get a glimpse of what may be on the floor of the coffin," Professor Harvardson said.

"Shouldn't we wait for Abdul to be here?" a colleague
said, referring to Harvardson's Egyptian co-director
appointed by the Supreme Council of Antiquities.
"Abdul could be away for hours trying to secure the
mummy remains. Let's be realistic," Harvardson said.
"At any moment, maybe with a change of temperature, a
bump, or even more likely, with all this dust around, a
single sneeze, and this whole mummy base could shiver
into dust."
The mummy's remains, stretchered away by workers,
had been in the same poor state this coffin, the body
lying crumbled and flat as a destroyed city razed to the
ground.
"Maybe this really was the tomb of the god Seth, the
chaotic devil-god of the desert dust storms, returning to
the desert dust he once ruled," Harvardson said, half-
seriously. For the ancient Egyptians, the gods could also
die, he recalled, and so they were frequently represented
as mummiform and were known to possess burial sites
in places throughout Egypt.
There had been great speculation by the press after the
discovery. Headlines dubbed the treasures 'The Golden
Tomb of the Devil God Seth', likening the find to tombs
in Abydos and Saqqara that were said to be symbolic
tombs of the god Osiris. Professor Harvardson had
taken a more conservative view, identifying the tomb
owner as most likely a high priest of Seth of maybe even
an unknown Sethian Priest-King, but it would be ironic
if the tomb owner were something more than that and
science never guessed it, he thought.
"Oh for the early days of buccaneering archaeology,
Friends," he said, "when Finders Keepers operated, or at
least a fifty-fifty division of the spoils. After all the
fanfare and heady excitement, the treasures are carted
away and all we get left with are ashes," he said.
"And credit, don't forget, which is not going to harm our
academic careers."

"Ah yes, the glory, but nothing to show for it, least of all gold. Maybe we should each grab a pocketful of Seth's god-dust before it goes too."

The careful, gloved finger of Nadine drew back the cloth that stuck to the ancient wooden baseboard and it came away to reveal markings beneath.

Texts?

That great hope of archaeologists vanished as they looked more closely.

Illustrations.

A map.

"An early map of the Book of the Two Ways."

The Book of Two Ways appeared over four thousand years ago and were the oldest illustrated books in history, coloured drawings of maps on the floor of coffins. They were ritual landscapes of roads through the underworld. Featuring illustrated demon animals to avoid along the route, they acted as a magical guide for the soul on their journey to Egyptian eternity. *As for those who know them (the two ways), they shall find their paths'* it was said of these esoteric guides.

Professor Harvardson was a leading expert on the Egyptian underworld and what the others took to be a map of the underworld he saw as something more startling.

"Shine more light down here." He bent low to inspect the map closely. "Stand dead still and don't even breathe," he said.

He dug an iPhone out of a trouser pocket and with a trembling finger opened the camera icon.

The camera image of the rotting coffin floor swelled in the screen. He enlarged it, tapped the button repeatedly, stopped, checked the images were saved, went closer, took more shots.

"Good, we've recorded it," someone said.

"What now?"

Professor Harvardson carefully slid the iPhone back into the safety of his pocket.

"This."
He raised his fists. He brought them down, smashing the crumbled wood. Pulverizing it. Repeatedly.
Under the shocked eyes of his team.
"Have you gone mad?"
"What the hell are you doing, David?"
He brushed the dust flat, making dozers of his palms.
"There, it never existed. And none of you must ever say otherwise."
Satisfied with its utter demolishment, Harvardson slapped the powder off his hands like a weightlifter after a successful lift.
"This, Friends, will be our great secret, a secret that will change our fortunes one day, when all the dust has settled years from now."

Aswan Lake crocodiles on show

CHAPTER 5

May you drown and the crocodile be against you

The next morning the cruise boat stopped for a visit to the ancient temples of Amada and Derr and a tomb of a Viceroy of Nubia on the shore of Lake Nasser.

Daniel and Kate joined the line of passengers who had chosen to go ashore, ferried in launches with armed guards aboard, that drew up in the shallows. One at a time they walked a plank to the shore, teetering along narrow, ribbed lengths, while crewmembers held up a pole as a makeshift handrail to steady their progress.

"Amazingly, nobody drowned or even got their feet wet," Daniel said.

Local villagers appeared on the scene, sporting live baby crocodiles with taped jaws for the visitors' cameras.

"You mean there are crocodiles in here?" Kate said, dark eyes widening. "I would never have walked the plank so casually."

"Estimates put Lake Nasser's crocodile population in the hundreds," Daniel said.

Egyptian licensed guides took the visitors in groups for guided tours, while the older hands, including Jemma Karnak, went their own way.

"Another temple rescued from drowning in the lake," Daniel told her as they approached a squat stone structure that bulked in the desert sand. "Amada is the oldest temple in Nubia, built by Thutmosis the Third."

Nearby stood the temple of Derr, a rock cut sanctuary. "Like Abu Simbel, cut into blocks and moved up higher in a feat of engineering that might have impressed the pharaohs."

Though faded in places, painted reliefs still enlivened the walls of Amada. "Egypt, land of cats, but the

pharaohs were no pussycats," Daniel commented, pointing at a scene of carnage. "That's a later pharaoh Amenhotep the Second devastating the enemy. He tells how he personally executed a bunch of chieftains with his sword and hung their bodies from the prow of his boat as trophies."
They spotted some of the Dream Team inside the temple chambers, Professor Harvardson and his wife, and further on, one of the other archaeologists searching out features of interest.
They continued to the adjacent temple of Derr, built by Rameses the Great, cut into an original cliff and yet miraculously raised and surrounded by a new cliff of stone.
It was good to stretch the legs on firm ground, Daniel thought, observing groups of fellow passengers trailing in the slip-stream narration of their tour guides.

They were returning to the boat after their tour when an alarmed Randa brought the news.
A body had been found on the shoreline by locals.
One of the archaeologists of the Dream Team.
There had been no sign of reptilian attacks, however.
Maybe they had just found the body in time.
"The body has been in the water overnight," the Egyptian doctor concluded after an examination in his surgery, back on board the cruise boat. "There are signs of haematoma to the temple. Maybe a bang on the way down to the water," he said, avoiding the obvious suspicion.
A second death on the boat was making people nervous. No note accompanied this death, but the tomb-curse subtext was clear enough to Daniel.

May you drown and the crocodile be against you.

"From bad to worse! Now two fatalities, Daniel!" Khadir
said. "The members of a celebrated archaeology team
are clearly emerging as the targets of a killer."
"Life for the Dream Team is becoming a nightmare,"
Daniel said.
It was no less a nightmare for the Supreme Council of
Antiquities official. To match the vast ears of Senusert
III, Khalid now bore the look of the aging king in later
representations, sagging granite jowls and brows heavy
with cares and disenchantment.
"What do we do?"
"Guard the remaining members on board," Daniel
suggested.
"Yes, we will post discreet watchers on their cabins for
the remainder of the cruise. Does this bring you any
closer to an answer?"
"It does focus my mind. This is not the work of some
serial killer murdering archaeologists at random. I'll
examine the man's cabin for any clues. Not that I really
expect to find anything there."

"I've been looking for you," Jemma Karnak said,
tracking him down to the dead man's cabin as he
emerged after completing a fruitless search for evidence.
"This changes everything, don't you think? Another
murder - and now a pattern."
"Murder?"
"You think a goat-footed archaeologist like Terence just
toppled over a rail?"
"How can I help you, Jemma?"
"Maybe I can help you. I last saw the dead man Terence
in the bar last night, locked in mortal and boozy
conversation with that journalist who interviewed me.
Maybe a quiet chat with her could be helpful to your
investigation."
"Thank you. You know, I can conceive of hostility
towards archaeologists from certain extremist quarters,

but why attack the Dream Team? Because they have the highest profiles right now?”
“Or maybe because they have a secret and someone wants to silence them. I’ve often wondered why they slammed the door on me like that. It was as if they wanted to keep something from me.”
“A secret? Their find was splashed all over the news.”
“Even so. There is something we don’t know.”

“You’re just the person I’ve been wanting to interview,” the journalist said to Daniel.
Gail was a breezy travel writer for the Guardian and they met over coffee on the sundeck under a canvas awning.
“Actually no, I’m the one who wants to interview you,” he said.
She laughed.
“Let’s have duelling interviews.”
“I understand that you had a deep and meaningful chat last night with the archaeologist who went missing. I’m sure journalistic confidentiality doesn’t apply to enticing travel writing. So tell me, what did he talk about?”
“Here’s what I don’t get. Why are you, the cruise Egyptologist, running an investigation, asking questions?’
“As the appointed cruise Egyptologist, I am helping authorities with their enquiries.”
“In journo-code, helping with enquiries means you’re a suspect.”
“I make a suspect detective, perhaps, but I’m doing my best to establish the facts. Now, the question.”
“Yes, the question, why you? Is it because of your involvement in the mock-murder mystery cruise case that we all read about? Do the authorities now regard you as a sleuth for hire?”
“No, I mean *my* question. What did the archaeologist talk to you about?”

"Oh, that. He appeared to be a frightened man, frankly.
Kept hinting at some explosive secret he knew that
might be putting his life in danger. Mulled about writing
it down some time and if anything happened to him, it
could be sent to me - as the archaeological expose of the
century."
So there was a secret, Daniel thought, and a big one.
Jemma Karnak, the crime writer had worked that out.
She was one step ahead of him. Maybe he should turn
over this investigation to her, he thought with a stab of
self-doubt.
But that wasn't his agreement with the Egyptian
authorities.
You help us and we'll help you.

His next meeting with the Dream Team was a far
different affair, apart from depleted numbers.
The mood was no longer stony. It was tense.
Now there were only four. Professor Harvardson, Nadine
his youthful Egyptologist wife, the Egyptian co-director
of the dig, Abdul, and the epigraphic expert Carlton who
sat in the furthest chair from the couple.
"I'll ask it again. Do you feel under attack as
archaeologists?" Daniel said.
"You haven't worked out what happened to our first
colleague yet," Professor Harvardson said. "What chance
have you got of finding out the truth about this latest
accident?"
"Oh, so this was an accident?" Daniel said. "The
examination revealed a bump on his temple, which may
have happened in falling, or may not. But you say an
accident."
"It was never a bloody accident," the younger epigraphic
expert Carlton growled. "Terence didn't just go and jump
in the Lake."

"I don't have to be a detective to see a pattern here,"
Daniel said. "Someone wants to ruin your party. Is it
because they want to shut you up? Is there something
the world doesn't know about you? Some precious
secret from the last dig? Something hidden away?"
That got eyes hardening, people subtly tensing.
"There's no secret. Everything precious on that dig is
right there on display in the new Grand Egyptian
Museum in Saqqara," Harvardson said. "The days of
slipping a treasure or two away under the nose of
Antiquities is well and truly over."
"That's what I would have thought, so it's puzzling."
"So puzzle away."
"If it is any comfort, this is all a mystery to me, too," the
Egyptian co-director Abdul said with a note of sympathy
for Daniel.

A comfortable navigating position belied a skillful captain

Ahmed Khalid of the Supreme Council of Antiquities
was a worried man.

The visage of Khadir had progressed from a look of aging
like the later statues of Pharaoh Senusert III statues to
crumbling in despair.

They met alone in the Boat Manager's office.

"If you love Egypt, Daniel, find us answers," Khalid said.
"The future of our struggling nation's international
reputation is at stake. We can only stop this disaster
from growing if we find out who is the culprit. If you
have even the faintest suspicions of their identity, tell
me. We will lock them up, detain them in their cabins
until the end of the cruise at Aswan to be safe."

"You'd have to lock them all up to be safe. I still don't
know the answer yet."

"Then it is vital we continue as normal. You are
scheduled to give another guest lecture to the
passengers today. Perhaps make it an address on a
more positive note, My Friend."

"The Great Return to Egypt," Daniel announced to his
audience of passengers in the cruise boat lounge room.
Amazingly, whispers of mishaps among archaeologists
onboard had not deterred his audience of Egypt lovers,
only sharpened their interest.

A good-sized turnout faced him from the spread of
comfortable chairs arranged about the room.

Jemma Karnak and Kate were there, along with the SCA
people, but the Dream Team had decided to sit this one
out, all except for one of their members, the young wife
Nadine, who slipped in just as he was about to begin,
and took a seat at the back. A spy? Keeping an eye on
an adversary?

"The Return theme echoes a charming tale in Egyptian
mythology called The Return of the Wandering
Goddess," Daniel said. "A story set right here in Nubia.
At our next stop, among a cluster of temples at Wadi es-

Sebua, you will visit the great temple of Dakka.
Here, the players in this drama, a lioness-goddess and a baboon, can be seen carved in relief on a stone wall." He flashed up a photograph on a screen of a baboon in an attitude of reverence standing in front of a lioness.

"These characters are also the stars of an operatic production that will take place in Philae after the first day of the congress.
Every year in ancient times, worshipers celebrated the important Festival of the Wandering Goddess at temples all the way from Dakka in Nubia, to Dendera in Egypt, culminating on the island Temple of Philae, festivities involving processions, music, dancing and revelry.
The event originated when the goddess, daughter of the sun god Re, in the form of a mighty lioness, took exception to Egypt, and, like international tourism, turned her back on the place. She abandoned Egypt and wandered off in a huff, like a whirlwind, into the deserts of Nubia. This alarmed her father, the god Re, because, like a tourism economy without foreign currency, ancient Egypt was vulnerable without the power of the

goddess. So Re sent the god of wisdom, Thoth, into Nubia to track her down and bring her back.

Thoth, often depicted as a man with the head of an ibis, could also appear in the form of a baboon, and for this mission, he decided to assume the guise of the ape, thinking: "Who can be angry with a little monkey?"

Well, an angry goddess could be, as he discovered.

He set off after the lioness-goddess, taking with him loads of provisions and offerings to soothe her anger and lure her back, probably loaded on the backs of pack animals, donkeys in those days, since camels only came on the scene later in Egypt's history.

After many days of trekking across the hot sands, Thoth caught up with the wandering goddess in the middle of the Sahara, probably as far south as Abu Simbel's, location today.

"Why are you following me?" the goddess said.

Thoth knew that in this moment of confronting the lioness he was in peril.

How do you appease a ferocious goddess and stop her from biting your head off? You'd better be damned interesting.

Thoth knew what the goddess liked.

"Turn back, Great Goddess. I have come to escort you back to Egypt and I have wondrous tales to tell you along the way," the Thoth baboon said.

"You see, Daniel said, "it's my theory that this drama was a forerunner of One Thousand and One Nights, the

Arabian Nights classic where the beautiful and clever
Shehezerade avoided execution by a murderous King.
The story goes that this king had a problem. He'd
caught his first wife being unfaithful to him and so he
swore to have a new wife each day and behead the old
one at dawn. Night after night, Shehezerade strung the
king along with a series of cliffhanger stories, prolonging
her life by delaying execution. The little trickster
baboon, like the future Shehezerade, planned to spin a
string of stories, drawing the lioness step by step across
the desert, charming her all back to Mother Egypt, just
as modern Egypt is trying to charm tourists back
today."
"You think words can turn my head?" the goddess
growled. "I am weary of words and praises."
"Tales about you."
"Even so."
The baboon decided to reach for more ammunition,
which he'd wisely brought along.
"As well as diverting tales, I have also brought tempting
offerings to give you along the way, gifts, precious
objects..."
"Foolish baboon! Do you think I can be tempted with
trinkets? What have you got?"
He had come prepared.
"A mirror."
The lioness-goddess roared, but not with laughter.
Anger.
"Cheap mirrors and beads may dazzle the wild Kushite
tribes people, but not a goddess. What sort of mirror?"
"This one." He produced a splendid gold and electrum
mirror bearing a handle in the shape of Hathor.
"A divine mirror that reflects like the beauty of the
moon, where you can admire your beauty at its most
sublime."
Naturally, she was intrigued.

Soon they were walking back together, the goddess
pausing only to take long admiring glances at her
beauty in the mirror, which he held up for her.
Thoth launched into his tales to keep her amused along
the journey, and at any sign of flagging interest on her
part, he plied her with costly fragrances, jars of wine
and chocolate. Well, not chocolate in ancient Egypt.
Cakes sweetened with dates and honey most likely.
Basically, everything a goddess could want.
Until finally, many a tale later, Thoth led the goddess
back for a happy return to Egypt, ending in a festival
procession at Philae Island Temple. The order of the

universe had been restored and the people were jubilant..."

Return of the wandering goddess

Daniel took a pensive tour of the boat with the guidance
of Randa, in search of... what?
An idea?
First they covered the decks, hoping to find signs that
the drowned man had been involved in a struggle before
falling overboard. Then they progressed to the
staterooms and lounges.
Daniel even checked out the vantage point of the cruise
boat captain, a cheery man in a *galabeya* whose
comfortable navigating style, while squatting on the
cushion of a lounge chair in front of his controls, belied
his skills.

Daniel and Kate had lunch together in the turn of the
century dining room while the cruise boat sailed on.
Jemma Karnak joined them at the meal.
"Was the journalist helpful?" she asked him.
"She confirmed what you suspected. I bow to your
superior author's instinct. Something is being hidden.
There's a secret around the Dream Team that the world
has yet to discover."
"And maybe one that somebody wants to stop the world
from ever finding out about."
"Tell me more about your early work with Professor
Harvardson," he said
"In those early days - before the designation of an
archaeological Dream Team even arose - we
concentrated our work in the region of Kom Ombo and
Wadi Hammamat, the pharaonic route to the eastern
desert, source of stone for the royal monuments, and,
most importantly, for gold, with gold mine settlement
dotting the route. You'll undoubtedly know about the
Turin Papyrus Map showing part of the Wadi
Hammamat."
"It's the oldest map in history, depicting geological
features like pink and black hills still recognizable today
along a fifteen kilometre stretch of the route."

"Exactly, the golden artery to Kom Ombo that earned it the title of 'City of Gold'. Rivers of gold flowed into Egypt from Wadi Hammamat, as they also did from Nubia of course, and this seemed a perfect site for a golden tomb in Egypt."

"Rivers of gold is a good description of the precious metal in ancient Egypt," Daniel agreed. "Thutmosis alone gave fourteen tons of gold to the Amun temple. And one pharaoh, Osorkon, of Libyan descent, made gifts to various temples of twenty-five tons of gold. No wonder Egyptians needed to keep a wary look out over their shoulders for envious and looting empires like the Assyrians and Persians."

"True. But I don't know how all this helps you, Daniel. I wish I could dream up a brilliant plot solution for you."

"You confessed in your book-signing message to Kate that you won't go on writing murder mysteries forever. What would you do in place of it, apart from living high on your royalties?"

"I can't imagine. It's too late to go back to archaeology now. Maybe I could become a kind of cruise Egyptologist like you, or Writer-in-ship-board-Residence and take groups of my murder mystery readers on tours of all the archaeological sites of Egypt that have appeared in my books. It might remind me of some of the places, stories and characters I've forgotten about. I sometimes think my readers know my books better than I do."

"I mostly read non fiction."

"So I could put you in an Egypt murder mystery book of mine and you'd never know it."

"Maybe I'm in one of yours now and you're penning my struggling investigation."

"Ooh, I like that."

"I'm not sure I would. I feel unable to control events as it is."

"How are you finding the crossover from Egyptology to crime detection?" Jemma said.

"It's not something I would have chosen. There's enough mystery for me in ancient Egypt without adding murder mystery. Relics and ruins give me answers, people, more questions. Similarities? It's well known that both Egyptology and detective work require digging below the surface in order to get to the facts and the truth. Except all the witnesses are dead in archaeology. What about you?"

"It was hard for me to give away archaeology. I suppose by writing so many books I was trying to shake off something."

Their cruise boat remained in the waters of Amada for dinner and overnight.

Housekeeping, after servicing the cabin, had left a sinister surprise for Daniel and Kate lying on their bed. Kate gasped and gave startled jump as they came inside.

The curling forms of a pair of massive Egyptian cobras reared up on the bed cover, jaws apart to strike.

"Don't be afraid," Daniel said in a murmur. "If you look closely, those cobras are snowy white, not a natural tone, and their snakeskin is actually terry towel. Origami towel snakes. Housekeeping staff on cruise boats like to be creative with guests and fold these clever cruise boat animals out of towels. Along with the petal eyes, I rather like the pink flowers in their jaws, fanning their mouths open like exposed fangs."

"What a shame to destroy them!"

"Yes, but more of a shame if they'd been real and destroyed us."

"All the same," she said. "I'll certainly be checking between the sheets before bed tonight. Scorpions, baby crocodiles and now snakes. Enough Nubian creatures to give me nightmares."

"Going through a patch of self doubt?" Kate said later as they lay in the bed.

"I'm probably questioning myself more than I'm questioning suspects."

"It sounds as if Jemma Karnak is trying to out-plot you. She's very good at it, don't forget. She's been doing it for years. I don't know how she dreams up new plot permutations with each book. I can't pick her killer."

"Nor me mine. Any idea about who's bumping off members of my profession?"

"No, but it bothers me that you never worry about being a target yourself."

"What makes you say that?"

"You never check between the sheets."

"Then I'd better not do any leaning over deck rails either."

"Don't. You're making me nervous."

"You started it."

"I sometimes feel the eyes of the world are on us, watching this celebration cruise - and the Great Return to Egypt event in Philae to follow. I'd hate a scandal to spoil things for Egypt."

"Not you, too. Our friend Khadir from the SCA has already placed the future of Egypt's tourism and economy on my shoulders and it feels like the weight of the pyramids."

Valley of the Lions, Wadi es-Sebua Temple

Fallen Rameses outside the temple precinct

CHAPTER 6
The mighty fallen

The fallen stone statue of Rameses the Great lay flat on its back in the red desert sand, clutching an emblematic stave at its side, sightless eyes staring up at the glare of an azure Nubian sky.

"Fallen Rameses. All that might and glory toppled in the dust," Daniel commented as he stood with Kate, the SCA woman Randa and the author Jemma Karnak.

The cruise boat had stopped in the middle of the Sahara Desert for a visit to the Wadi es-Sebua temple complex. The official organizers were intent on following the planned itinerary and keeping the situation as normal as possible. The temples needed a full day to explore, the itinerary suggested.

Unlike the Nile Valley, where ancient temples lay scattered along a thousand miles of the river, three Nubian temples lay clustered here, saved from drowning in the rising waters of the Aswan Dam - the temples of Wadi es-Sebua, Dakka and smaller temple of Maharraka.

The passengers began their tour with the atmospheric New Kingdom temple of Wadi es-Sebua.

They passed through an avenue of eight stone sphinxes guarding the entrance, the rows of creatures strikingly echoed by a long line of reclining camels outside the precinct, waiting to transport visitors to the next attraction, the soaring pylons of the Dakka Temple that rose on a bluff in the distance.

While some chose to climb on the camel train, others decided to make the trek on foot. The vast Temple of Dakka, built in the Ptolemaic era, lay at the end of a sweeping desert embankment and from where they stood, its almost forty-feet high pylons dominating the skyline

As well as the sphinxes guarding the complex of temples, Daniel noticed a stronger than usual presence of armed security.
Randa explained
"You may have noticed the greater numbers of armed guards here," she said. "After the twenty-eleven revolution, the temples were left without guards and looting was reported, so they are here to prevent further attempts."
Armed guards might stop looters and even dissidents, but they could not protect passengers from each other.

The archaeologist climbed alone up steps to the top of the pylon of Dakka Temple and paused to soak in the view from above.
The vista took his breath away.
The winking lapis-lazuli of the lake, the carnelian redness of the rocky desert and the temples standing out like cut-rock gems against the background.
He marvelled that this temple and its pylons, dedicated to the God Thoth, had been moved forty kilometres upstream to escape the deluge of the Aswan High Dam.
The kilometre walk here had been worth it and the climb up the pylon steps.
Was that a welcome breeze touching his back?
Why in one spot?
A focused pressure concentrated in the middle of his spine
Too late he felt a violent shove.
It propelled him bodily into the yawning desert scene.
It took his breath away again.

A great archaeologist fallen.
Daniel wondered.

What might be the tomb-curse subtext behind Professor
Harvardson's death?
Perhaps...

May you fall like Apophis to the anger of Re

They found the bearded archaeologist lying face up,
sightless eyes directed at the sky, like an emulation of
the fallen statue of Rameses that lay toppled in the red
desert sand near the Wadi es-Sebua Temple precinct.
"Death for this man was instantaneous," the Egyptian
boat doctor said, after an examination in the boat's
surgery. "The back of his head struck stone."
"Facing up? Does that mean he toppled backwards from
the pylon?"
The doctor shrugged.
"He may have toppled and tumbled over."
"Pushed from behind? A fall seems an unlikely accident
for a skilled archaeologist accustomed to negotiating
tombs, cliffs and ruins. And where was his wife Nadine
at the time? They were together earlier."
"Not in this case," Khadir said. "And I am afraid it is
partly your fault."
"My fault?"
"I spoke to her after the tragedy and she said she had
been tired after the long walk to Dakka and left
Professor Harvardson to climb up the steps of the pylon
alone. She wanted to examine the wall relief of the
wandering lioness goddess and the baboon - inspired by
your presentation to the passengers."
A compliment, Daniel thought.
Perhaps.
"Three world-famous archaeologists dead!" The world-
weary, pharaonic visage of Khadir hung in despair.
"This cruise boat has become a morgue and tomorrow
we set sail for Aswan, with just one short stop on the
way. Our international event lies in ruins."

Like my career as an archaeologist detective, Daniel
thought.
The pyramids weighing on Daniel's shoulders suddenly
took on the weight of the Giza Plateau.
He had failed and was running out of cruise days.
He recalled spotting Harvardson and his wife only once
at Wadi es-Sebua, next to a stone sphinx, a lion's body
with the pharaonic head of Rameses.
"Rameses, lionised," Daniel had commented to
Harvardson who was inspecting the sphinx. "I'm sure
you know the feeling."
Now a third death had happened. On his watch. And he
had been unable to stop it, difficult as that task might
have been with a concentration of temples to keep an
eye on.
A group of three temples.
And now there were three archaeologists left in the
Dream Team.
The group had been reduced to Nadine, the shaken
young Egyptologist wife of the Professor, the epigraphic
expert Carlton, and finally the Egyptian co-director,
Abdul.
A group of archaeologists. A group of temples.
It sparked a thought.
Maybe these murders were a group affair. Not an attack
on a celebrated archaeology team by some outsider, but
a bitter elimination struggle between members of the
group.
"We may not have failed yet," Daniel said.
Khedive looked astounded.
"You think I can explain away three murders - of three
famous archaeologists - to the international
community?"
"Yes. If I can prove that it was a feud between
archaeologists. Homicide happens. It's not going to
frighten tourists away. That will only occur if there are
political or ideological forces at work."

"But why would this team attack each other? They have covered themselves in glory and are keynote delegates at the Philae Congress."
"Jealousy? A fight over a bigger share of glory? Maybe. But I think it could be a fight for a share of something bigger. I believe it has to do with a secret they share."
"You mean something hidden - antiquities?"
"I'm not sure."
Khalid shook his head.
"I know the Egyptian co-director of the dig, Abdul, an honest family man. I cannot believe he would be involved in illegal activity."
"Maybe he isn't. Maybe they kept Abdul - and others - out of the loop."
"Then what do we do from here? Will they go on murdering each other until the last man standing? I should confine the last two suspects to their cabins until the end of the cruise. For their own safety and to avoid more fatalities."
"Then we may never find the proof that there's a conspiracy, or who the killer is. People will be left to think the worst. That extremists are behind these deaths in Nubia. I say we let it play out. We are forced to play a waiting game."

Daniel sought out the advice of crime author Jemma Karnak, visiting her in her cabin. He needed to talk to someone who spent their life weaving plots of murder and mayhem set in Egypt.
"I hope I've dropped lower down on your list of suspects, Daniel," she said, opening the door. "You'll recall that I was never out of your sight at Wadi es-Sebua." It was true, he thought. Jemma, along with Kate and Randa, had been with him the whole time at the cluster of temples. "How can I help?" she said.
"I want to sound you out on a plot scenario."

"Sorry, no. I make it a point never to discuss writers'
plot ideas with them. Gets you into legal trouble.
Kidding. Feel like a drink? Only Egyptian Beer, I'm
afraid. Following the ancients, you know."
"Beer is fine."
She poured them both a long glass and they sat
opposite each other with a view of the harbour of Wadi
es-Sebua filling a panoramic cabin window.
"I'm sorry about Harvardson," he said. "It must have
come as quite a shock to you. Just because someone is
out of your life and taken up with someone new doesn't
mean they're totally out of your feelings."
"I hated him," she said frankly. "Not because he ran off
with a neophyte Egyptologist. I hated him for taking *us*
away, taking away years of shared scholarship and
archaeological dreams. Women are supposed to be
emotional, but this is not an emotional hatred. It's a
cerebral hatred. Because I live the life of the mind, you
see, as I sense you do too."
He raised his glass.
"Here's to mutual hatreds. I hated him a bit too, I
confess, because he did something I may never achieve."
"And something he could not have achieved without me,
don't forget. But you didn't come here to offer grief
counselling. What's on your mind, Daniel?"
He couldn't lie.
He told her the status of his thinking.
She arched those Nefertiti eyebrows.
"You've made a leap. Who do you suspect? Rivalry and
greed provide a powerful motive for murder and it feeds
into the scenario that their exists some valuable and
guarded secret between them. Maybe they had a row."
"We can probably rule out the Egyptian co-director
Abdul at this stage. Khalid has a high opinion of his
probity. That only leaves Nadine and Carlton, the
epigraphic expert. Most likely Carlton took action
against Harvardson. Maybe he blamed him for the
killings and it was a pre-emptive strike."

"He thought David was the killer? Well, my ex-husband was a ruthless character, as our discarded relationship proved. And he was always materialistic. A tendency strengthened by trying to keep an expensive young wife happy, no doubt. So who killed the others?"
Daniel gave a sigh.
"I suppose Carlton the epigraphic expert may have been the killer all along. Remember that note that came with the first death by scorpions. Tomb Robber, may the scorpions' stings be against you and your greed, and strike with the fire of the god's anger. As an epigrapher, Carlton would be an expert on tomb inscriptions and know their pattern. The note may have been an attempt to throw everybody off the scent."
"What about David's new wife, or should I say widow? She was ruthless too, as she proved by destroying my marriage and shouldn't be underestimated in spite of her clinging-vine manner."
"Perhaps, but the violence of the drowning and the shove from the top of a temple pylon don't quite seem like the murder methods of choice for a woman."
"Female archaeologists, accustomed to the rigours of archaeological digs, are a lot more physical than you give them credit for. They need to be."
"That's true. But it would probably have taken the force of a man to shove him off like that. Women prefer more indirect means like poison. Women are more subtle."
"Thank you. Unless of course the clingy-wife manner was all an act and Nadine is actually in it with Carlton, a much younger man," Jemma said.
"You see why I wanted to talk to you. You weave complicated plots for a living. The trouble is, even if Carlton is my main suspect, we still can't prove a motive. It's only a suspicion at this stage that the team was sharing a secret. We've got to establish that secret, find what could drive supposedly-civilized academics to murder."

"We? So I'm on your team now, working on a real life murder mystery?"

"It appears so."

"How thrilling. I'm so glad I came back to Lake Nasser on another cruise."

"So you've been here before?"

"On this very boat. What are you going to do now? Are you planning to interrogate the suspects?"

"Not sure. Maybe give them rope."

"*Halfa* grass rope?" she said.

Gallows' humour.

The murder writer in her.

CHAPTER 7
Last leg of the cruise

"I have spoken again with the young widow Egyptologist," Khalid told Daniel.
"Has she fallen apart?"
"Surprisingly, no. She is a stronger young lady than we might have imagined. Distraught, of course. But, surprisingly, she is quite prepared to go on to Philae and deliver Professor Harvardson's paper at the Congress."
"I suppose we should give her credit for that."
"She wanted to get to grips with his material right away. She asked if the Boat Manager could unlock the cabin's safety box where Harvardson kept his laptop for security."
"Nadine didn't have access herself? His wife?"
"Apparently, not."
"He liked to keep his presentation to himself?"
Khalid shrugged.
"She was quite diligent and went straight to work on a presentation rehearsal. Fortunately she knew the password for his laptop. The Philae open-air congress is rushing up at us."
"What about Carlton?"
"Not saying much, but a tense man. Yet he too is staying the course and going on to our Philae Congress."
"*Hm.* Maybe because cutting and running now might look suspicious. And he may be hanging around for a pay off."
"What possible pay-off? What secret could they be keeping?"
"Maybe the clue lies inside Harvardson's laptop that he so cautiously locked away. Maybe you should interrupt her rehearsals and impound the laptop for a while,

citing it as possible material evidence in the
investigation into her husband's death."

It was cocktails at sunset.
Kate took a cocktail and circulated among the guests on
the shaded sundeck.
The American Biblical archaeology sponsor caught her
eye. She'd met him briefly when Daniel had taken the
man aside to question him. He stood with a private
security detachment around him. Two strapping young
men like sidesmen in a cult church.
"You look doubly relaxed with that umbrella cocktail in
your hand, while posed under a shaded deck," she said.
"Relaxed?" The sponsor's golden glasses flashed and his
washed-out blue eyes behind rolled, showing the whites,
which gave him a look of religious terror. "I would say
instead that I feel doubly vindicated, no triply so,
following three deaths among those who unleashed the
evil of the Golden Seth tomb on the world. Believe me,
the demonic malignancy of that tomb will only continue
to spread its poison in a cycle of death. Seth, the
Egyptian entity, was the devil of ancient Egypt, let us
recall."
"Sad for the three archaeologists though," she said. "I
can't believe they deserved to suffer those terrible
accidents."
"No? Scripture says: 'Against all the gods of Egypt I will
execute judgment: I am the Lord. The Bible also tells us
that we wrestle not against flesh and blood, but against
principalities, against powers, against the rulers of the
darkness of this world."
"But wait, are you saying that God punished them, or
that some malignancy in the tomb was to blame?"
"I'll let you decide."
Had he, or his young minders, given God a little help in
executing divine punishment?

A chill passed through Kate.

She must alert Daniel to her fears.

Next she sought out a woman dressed in a crimped white Egyptian cotton gown with an Egyptian style broad collar necklace of turquoise around her throat, who styled herself as an Egyptian High Priestess of a European Kemetic Church.

Kate avoided a joke about fancy dress, a feature of many Egyptian cruises.

"Love your Egyptian cotton," she said.

"Thank you. White was a symbol of purity among priests and priestesses. They were forbidden to touch wool, though. They also washed their bodies twice a day as an act of purification."

"In this Nubian heat it's an act of survival."

"And shaved off their body hair too. All of it."

This was getting more personal than she cared for. Kate decided to probe her about the deaths of the archaeologists.

"I hope the string of unlucky accidents hasn't unsettled you."

The Kemetic priestess shook her arm and made a clutch of amulets rattle. Kate spotted a knot of Isis, a scarab, and an *ankh* cross. "That's why I wear these. And I see you wear the symbol of Maat around your neck." The woman's green malachite eyes questioned her. "The goddess of Truth and Justice."

"A gift from my boyfriend."

"Do you have an affinity for Egyptian mythology and symbolism?"

"Yes, not that I'd switch religions or anything."

"The intruders released powerful forces by entering the tomb, forces they did not know how to control. They are paying the price now."

Professor Harvardson's laptop was like a *MacBook of the Dead.*

Going into a dead man's electronic sanctuary was a little like intruding into his tomb, Daniel thought, opening the old-gold Apple MacBook at a desk in in the privacy of his own cabin, while Kate mixed with passengers on deck for cocktails-at-sunset.

Here on the laptop's screen arose the memories of a life stored on electronic walls, all the writings, all the treasures, all the victories and honours achieved.

Professor Harvardson had amassed a hoard.

Daniel could almost feel the dead man stirring as the footsteps of a stranger walked through his sanctuary. He began by scanning the text of the academic's forthcoming paper about the discovery of the golden Seth Tomb and a review of its ongoing impact on Egyptology. He saw photos of the undulating rocky Wadi Hammamat area where the tomb had been found and the chambers of the tomb crammed with funerary goods.

The snarling golden Seth mask, shrines, caskets, a golden trove that rivaled Howard Carter's discoveries of Tutankhamun in the Valley of the Kings or the golden and silver treasures uncovered by French Egyptologist Pierre Montet in *the Royal Necropolis of Tanis before the outbreak of World War II.*

Images that had been splashed across the screens and pages of the world's news media.

Daniel had become increasingly accustomed to conducting computer-based research instead of poring over printed books. Over the years he had collected a vast library of Egyptological books and they had become a treasure that he'd thought he'd never part with. So precious, he whimsically dreamed of being buried with his library one day, like a pharaoh with his tomb treasure.

But you couldn't take it with you in this life or the next, he'd decided and as he traveled more and more to Egypt, funding his research for his writing by working as a guest Egyptologist on cruises, he began to question

the value of his library. Yes, books were lovely things, artefacts in themselves, and old books smelled like papyrus, ink and archaeological dust, but they went out of date. Scholarship moved along and electronic books alone could keep up. They were perfect for the quicksilver nature of new ideas. So he'd sold off the bulk of his library, keeping just a few volumes for sentimental purposes, like *A Dictionary of Ancient Egyptian Civilization* by Georges Posener, the first book he'd ever bought for himself as a schoolboy, after winning prize money in a nationwide schools essay competition, and also a copy of the first book his mother had bought him, Sir Alan Gardiner's *Egypt of the Pharaohs,* encouraging his passion for Egypt.
Electronic books were living things, ever-refreshed electrons that paper, and even papyrus, could never achieve. In fact there was some of the permanence about e-books that he admired in the ancient Egyptian civilization itself. They never went out of print. They never yellowed, faded, gathered mildew, dust and eventually rotted.
He could read them at the bottom of a tomb and never have to angle a lamp just right.
He could live a mobile life *and* still have his books. They didn't smell like printed books, true, but neither did they smell of dust mites...
Daniel moved on through the man's photo library. Professor Harvardson certainly had a fondness for gold. Golden masks, vases, shrines popped up everywhere among more perishable wooden items like a crumbled coffin that had an illustrated map of the underworld painted on its floor. The underworld was Harvardson's specialty, and, ironically, the underworld of illicit antiquity trading might well have been in his future plans.
Too much to study properly now, Daniel decided.

The bereaved young wife, keen to rehearse her Philae presentation, might demand the laptop back at any time.

Daniel dumped the photographs of the Seth dig onto a memory stick to keep and examine later.

Neither the young widow, not the epigrapher Carlton turned up for dinner in the boat's columned, vintage-style dining room.

A sign of something.

Grief, shock... guilt?

"How were cocktails at sunset?" he said, including Jemma Karnak in his questioning glance.

"I thought it was time to play Bond-girl and do a bit of spying, or at least snooping around to help you," Kate said. "I cornered that Biblical archaeology sponsor. His attitude was a concern, I must tell you."

After dinner, Daniel and his two companions hung around the cocktail bar area in the hope that the bereaved young wife and the epigraphic archaeologist might turn up.

"Do you believe in malignant forces?" Kate asked him.

"*I* do, my ex-mother in law," Jemma Karnak cut in.

"Me? I'm not slamming the door on any spiritual possibilities," Daniel said, "including the probability that there is a god. I think it's a paucity of imagination that stops many people believing, including the insufferable dread that they might be held accountable."

"The Bible archaeology man was unnerving and so was that Kemetic priestess," Kate said.

"You're stoking my fears. What if I'm going down the wrong track and running out of time? Tomorrow evening we reach Aswan and the cruise ends."

In the morning they began the nine-hour sail to Aswan.

Dinner and Overnight in Aswan, the itinerary said. *Then after Breakfast, Disembarkation and Transfer to the Old Cataract Hotel.*

The Congress was due to start the following day, held on the magical Island of Philae.

To Daniel's relief, and his growing dismay, nothing out of the ordinary occurred as the morning dragged on.

The newly widowed Nadine and the archaeologist Carlton made brief, but separate showings at breakfast. No mutual comforting after the shock of Professor Harvardson's death, he noted.

The passengers celebrated the crossing of the Tropic of Cancer during the day and congregated on deck for cocktails, with no sign of the young widow or the epigraphic expert.

Daniel felt he was crossing another line from success into failure.

Lunch on board of grilled Nile perch was succulently prepared, yet Daniel ate as if lost in a daze.

'Am I missing something?' he kept thinking over and over.

"No last minute hunches, Daniel?" Jemma Karnak said. "The kind my fictional detectives rely on?"

"More like last minute nagging doubts and fears."

"Well, you have a few hours and then there's our big congress at Philae."

"A gathering of the clans and fans of international Egyptology. Imagine if the real killer has gone undetected and he's going to be one of hundreds there. On the podium or maybe in the audience. How am I supposed to find him then?"

"The detective's difficulties ramp up, progress becomes impossible. That's good story development," Jemma said. "Builds up reader tension."

"No last minute hunches from you?" he said." You obviously keep coming up with solutions in your murder novels."

"I have one advantage. I know the end."

"Not me. How about an ending that leaves people hanging?"
"Unthinkable. My readers wouldn't stand for it."
Neither would his sponsor in Egyptian Antiquities.

Daniel skipped the visit to visit the final cluster of temples - Kalabsha Temple, Beit El Wali, and the Kiosk of Kertassi. If the young wife and the archaeologist were staying on board, so was he.
Kate went without him.
Under pressure from the widow, Khadir had felt compelled to return the Professor's laptop to Nadine.
She needed to familiarise herself with the contents and refusal to return her husband's presentation could put at risk the programme carefully planned by the Egyptian Ministry of Antiquities
Daniel wandered the boat.
He could see the salvaged temple complex from the deck, sitting perched on higher ground, dominated by the bulking structure of Kalabsha Temple and its two great pylons.
He kept an eye out for his two remaining suspects.

The salvaged Kalabsha temple complex within sight of Aswan

CHAPTER 8
Aswan

That night, berthed at their final destination of Aswan, the boat held a gala dinner on board to mark the last night of the cruise, an evening enlivened by Nubian music and dancers.

Maybe it was his mood, but it felt like an Egyptian tomb scene for Daniel and the pair of entwining female dancers in the chandelier-lit dining room reminded him of the Tomb of Nebamun fresco in the British Museum. Today's Muslim daughters of Nubian Egypt were rather more discreetly covered, however.

Tomb dancers

The young widow Nadine attended the gala dinner, with Carlton and the Egyptian co-director Abdul at her table, maybe to accustom herself to company again with the congress coming up.

How was she looking?

Composed and comfortable enough in her own presence, he decided, considering she no longer had Professor Harvardson to cling to.

Her resilience impressed him.

Grief? No black widow's weeds. Designer clothes and golden jewellery.

An alluring young sylph.

Jemma caught him staring.

"More *deben* for your thoughts."

"Your ex-husband had a classy taste in women, Jemma, both times. Do you feel any pity for her? Or resentment still?"

"If it hadn't been her it would have been some other bright-eyed PHD graduate back then." Jemma was resilient too. She raised her glass. "I'm sorry we can't be toasting your success tonight, Daniel. But there are still too many plot holes to fill. On the last night of the Murder in Nubia cruise you should be enacting some dramatic scene with all parties present. Like stopping the music and marching up there in front of the guests to share your labyrinthine process of deduction before the big reveal - the announcement of the identity of the killer of three famous archaeologists."

"Or plural. The killers. If they've been killing each other as I fear."

"Let's drink to an unfinished mystery then," she said.

"Maybe you can write a satisfying ending some day," he said.

"But it's your story."

"It's funny how your books are different, Jemma," Kate observed. "The detective always reveals the identity of the guilty party and their motive by the end of the story.

They're never stumped. Only real life detectives have cold cases, unsolved crimes that sit in folders for years."
"I hope mine isn't one of those," Daniel said.
"It would be tormenting, like suspecting the presence of a lost tomb and never making the discovery," Jemma said.

Back in their cabin, Daniel sat awake.
There was no sleeping on it, no hoping that a night's rest would make everything fall into place.
He sat at a desk in front of his laptop containing the downloaded photographs from Professor Harvardson's *MacBook of the Dead.*
A field director's personal record of the archaeological dig.
Kate spoke from the bed.
"Aren't we going to celebrate the last night of our cruise across the Sahara Desert on the Nubian Sea?"
Did she have to put it like that?

Daniel went back to the laptop and the photographs of the tomb treasures.
Gold everywhere. Untarnishable, eternal. The flesh of the gods, continually reborn in precious objects like golden masks, shrines, statues and jewellery. Glowing like the eternal sun, no matter how badly objects around them crumbled and decayed.
Harvardson could not get enough of golden images.
That was why the photographs of a rotted mummy baseboard with underworld diagrams on it stood out for Daniel. They showed traces of an unusually detailed map through an underworld, passing through mountains and desert. The Book of Ways. The oldest illustrated books in the world.
This one looked to be the very oldest.

Powdery and fragile. As if one breath could blow it away like desert dust.

Ash.

'All of my efforts seemed to be ending in that,' he thought.

While stuck on a cruise boat, his suspects were captive, still under his eye, specimens in a Petrie dish in theory at least. Here on the boat lay his best chance of finding the killer and proving the motive.

Once disembarked, they would be free to go their ways and cover their tracks.

Hotel of Agatha Christie's 'Death on the Nile'

CHAPTER 9

'Death on the Nile' hotel

Daniel was at a crossroads.
A crossroads of time and place.
Aswan, an oasis-like frontier town, had for thousands of years marked the borders between Egypt and Nubia. Here on a colossal outcrop of granite rock, the Nile's first cataract, stood the Old Cataract Hotel, itself an intersection of grand colonialism and palatial eastern opulence and it was his favourite hotel in Egypt.
It was also Jemma Karnak's delight.
"Crime fiction's hallowed ground," she commented to Daniel and Kate inside a palatial foyer vaulted by Moorish-style arches and columns and drooped with hanging chandeliers like the jewels of eastern paradise. "We walk in the footsteps of Agatha Christie. Over there on display is the bare mahogany desk where she sat and worked upstairs in Suite 1201, writing her beloved murder mystery Death on the Nile, and alongside it a wicker chair where she would recline and admire the sunsets from her balcony, weaving her plots. She could look down on the Nile, strewn with rocks and feluccas, and also view the archaeological ruins of Elephantine Island. The Old Cataract Hotel, at the gateway to Africa, was a palace for the Queen of crime fiction."
"And for a modern day rival who is intent on dethroning her," Daniel said.
"A pretender, let's say. Christie set some of her novel here during her sojourn of almost a year and she would relax on the terrace with cigar-chomping Winston Churchill. Today her ghost rubs shoulders with the ghosts of Czar Nicholas of Russia, Howard Carter, the Aga Khan, King Farouk, the Shah of Iran, Margaret Thatcher and Princess Diana.
"And, one day, with Jemma Karnak's ghost," Kate said.

"I'm not sure what I'll be remembered for."

"It clearly inspired you. Let's hope the hotel of Death on the Nile will give me some inspiration," Daniel said. "I didn't get a whole lot of help in Nubia."

"Speaking of help. Agatha Christie had an adviser, you know, an Egyptologists who helped her with the Egyptian elements in her writing, not to mention an archaeologist husband who specialised in ancient Middle Eastern history."

"While I have a writer to help me."

"Who was also once an archaeologist, remember. Yet I feel I'm in some kind of partnership with you Daniel, except that in this living mystery I am playing an active part and so it's more vivid for me than any of my books. I have never enjoyed crime so much."

Daniel saw the young widow Nadine checking in at the desk. The other archaeologists had checked in earlier. Tomorrow they would all vanish into a crowded congress on the island of Philae Temple.

"I hear the view from the Cataract Terrace is something to die for," Kate said.

"It is," Jemma said.

"Enough of dying perhaps," Daniel said. "At least for a while."

"Let's meet on the Terrace for a cooling drink, after we've settled into our rooms," Jemma said.

To die for?

Daniel sipped his beer while the two women drank in the view.

The Terrace of the Old Cataract Hotel was not a place to think about dying, Daniel reflected, heart-stopping as the view was. He wondered how Agatha could have dwelt on murder with the Nile swirling blue around granite rocks like elephant-backs and with the view of tilting white felucca sails altering their trigonometry as they tacked across the water, palms trees exploding in green bursts of fronds on the river banks.

But the ruins of the one-time fortress island of
Elephantine checked his reverie.
Ruins of archaeology.
That's where he'd started in this conscripted
investigation.
A career in ruins. It was not likely to be salvaged like
the threatened temples of Lake Nasser unless he made
some dramatic progress soon.
He stirred as he caught a glimpse of Nadine, the young
Egyptologist, and her colleague Carlton meeting up with
a pair of Egyptian men at a table further down the
terrace, having drinks and a sober conversation it
turned out.
Was she starting to mix with the congress crowd? He
wondered who they were. They looked like seasoned
types and were westernised in their clothing. Egyptian
archaeologists, he supposed.
Where was Abdul, the Egyptian co-director from the
team?
Kept out of the loop.
Khadir had probably been right when he'd doubted the
Egyptian's involvement in any nefarious busines

Jewel of the Nile

CHAPTER 10
Philae crescendo

"We need someone inside the tent of international archaeology at this event," the SCA man Ahmed Khadir had told him at the original briefing. He might have added 'marquee event'.

A flotilla of launches ferried the attendees across the still waters of the lower Aswan Dam reservoir to Philae, arriving at a giant marquee set up on the island of the temple complex dedicated to Isis, Hathor and numerous other deities. The temporary structure swallowed the Sound-and-Light seating area, soaring like an exhibition dome beside the stone walls, pylons and columns of Philae's temple complex, providing ample room for delegates to sit in spaced seating.

After the official opening speeches and lofty statements about a Great Return to Egypt that seemed to puff up the dome like a flame expanding a hot-air balloon, the programme began.

Daniel and Kate watched at the fringe as Egyptologist Nadine Harvardson presented her husband's paper over the speaker system.

She began a little nervously, but her young voice shook with passion as she delivered her dead husband's words.

"Many archaeologists will tell you that the treasure they hope to strike, should they penetrate the walls of an intact tomb, is not the rare and precious metal gold, but information, inscriptions, papyrus texts, history, reliefs that inform us about the past.

True.

And yet...

What shriveled soul does not want to discover the golden artistry of a Tutankhamun's mask, or the sublime beauty of a Nefertiti bust?

There was more in our tomb discovery than the language of words. The hoard of golden treasures spoke volumes - whole libraries - about Egyptian civilization and its artistry, symbolism and mind.
We found a tomb silent of all inscription and graphics, yet calling out to us like a trumpet fanfare down the long centuries... ”
Her fervor impressed the audience.
Daniel glanced at Jemma Karnak who raised a Nefertiti eyebrow.
A *deben* for her thoughts.
He turned a sweeping glance around the audience, recalling his conversation with Jemma.
“A gathering of the clans and fans of international Egyptology. Imagine if the real killer has gone undetected and he’s going to be one of hundreds there. On the podium or may be even in the audience. How am I supposed to find him then?”
“The detective’s difficulties ramp up, progress becomes impossible. That’s good story development,” Jemma said. “Builds up reader tension.”
“No last minute hunches from you if you keep coming on coming up with them in your novels?” he said.
“I have one advantage. I know the end.”
The end.
Ironically, the name Philae in Greek, or Pilak in ancient Egyptian, meant exactly that, ‘the end,’ the end of the navigable river before the rocky cataracts commenced. Was this the end for him, after a voyage of mystery across the Sahara on an inland sea, speeches and ripples of applause as a curtain came down?

He left Kate and Jemma and took a stroll through the great temple dedicated to Isis.
Like the temples in Nubia, this too had been transported to higher ground. In a joint operation over ten years, UNESCO and the Egyptian government had

moved it to this nearby island, which they bulldozed into the shape of the original one, but he could scarcely imagine it now.

He entered the stone-paved main courtyard lined by colonnades on either side, approaching the first temple pylon with its twin towers.

His murder investigation so far had been a little like this progression through the temple.

A beginning like this court, wide with possibilities, lined with colonnades like the boatload of possible suspects-to-be. Then the first pylon, decorated on one side with a scene of Ptolemy grasping the hair of a clutch of enemies and smashing in their skulls with his club. On the other side stood the sinuously carved image of the goddess.

The pylon bulked in front of Daniel like the confronting reality of the first murder, an archaeologist killed by the venom of seven deadly scorpions, a symbol of the goddess at the gate.

Tomb Robber, may the scorpions' stings be against you and your greed, and strike with the fire of the god's anger.

Then, a forecourt, and a second confronting murder.

May you drown and the crocodile be against you.

And then passing into the inner temple, dense with the mystery of columns and beyond, a pylon shaped doorway leading to the inner vestibule and the darkened sanctuaries of divinity, reminding him of the fallen idol of Rameses and of Professor Harvardson, the celebrated archaeologist, who had toppled to his doom.

May you fall like Apophis to the anger of Re.

More antechambers flanked him, but while the scale of the temple narrowed to the singular point of sacred gloom in the Sanctuary of Isis, Daniel had walked into total darkness in his investigation.

He had suspicions, but no proof of motive for murder. Proof in black and white.

Chipped in stone like the myriad texts and reliefs in the temple.

He scanned some of the texts, reflecting on the fact that the very last hieroglyph carved in Egypt happened here at Philae Temple. After the final ring of metal on stone, ancient Egypt fell silent...

And now the voice of the young widowed Egyptologist at the congress presentation rang in his memory...

"We found a tomb silent of all inscription and graphics, yet calling out to us like a trumpet fanfare down the long centuries..."

Empty of all inscription and graphics?

The thought jarred in his mind.

He remembered Harvardson's photograph of a crumbled wooden coffin base covered with illustrations, a rather unusual example of the world's oldest illustrated book, the Book of Two Ways, but this one had a peculiar map that showed geographical features, a road passing through coloured hills, like the Wadi Hammamat.

Was it a map of an ancient gold mine beyond Kom Ombo, the City of Gold?

Why had nobody ever spoken about it?

Was this the secret worth murdering for?

He'd have to examine the photograph on his laptop tonight when he returned to the hotel after the day's Congress.

The opening programme culminated in an evening of celebration, cocktails and snacks as the sunset made an envious flash on the beautiful stone temples of Philae. Then, as guests sat in chairs brought out from the Congress marquee, a major production swung into action, the staging of a newly composed opera for the occasion: *"The Return of the Wandering Goddess,"* performed by the Cairo Symphony orchestra and sung by a cast of Egyptian operatic singers.

Backed by floodlit Philae temples, the operatic cast arrived on the waters aboard divine golden barques, and they told the tale in operatic verse of the Return of the Wandering Goddess from the wilderness of Nubia and of the wily stratagems of the Thoth baboon.
The opera reached its crescendo when an Egyptian soprano, dressed as a lioness-woman, came on shore and entered the temple forecourt, trailing billowing white linen to be coaxed step by step towards the pyloned entrance by the Thoth baboon holding up a shining Hathor mirror like a moon.
A chorus of exultant priests and priestesses in white robes welcomed her arrival, singing:

Rejoice! She has turned her face North!
The wandering goddess has returned to Egypt!

An impressive production and imaginatively staged, Daniel thought, as he joined the audience in applause. It made him think of his own estrangement from archaeology and wonder if his journey back from Nubia might lead to a return of his passion.

A progression into mystery

214

A weary Kate curled up under the canopy of a four-poster bed in their hotel room, after a late formal dinner in the Old Cataract Hotel's grand '1920 Restaurant', a setting with Moorish arches and a spectacular domed ceiling like a mosque. There had been no sign of Nadine or Carlton at dinner, he'd noted.

Maybe they had chosen another of the three restaurant choices offered by the hotel.

Or perhaps the young woman had ordered room service, tired after her presentation at the Congress. He hadn't spotted her or the archaeologist Carlton at the opera.

Daniel opened up his laptop and set to work.

"How can you resist our four-poster bed?" Kate said, stifling a yawn.

Before he could answer, he heard Kate's sifted breathing in sleep.

Daniel found the image of the wooden coffin base among the laptop's photographs and enlarged it to full screen, eyes running over the map like an aerial satellite.

An echo of the famous Turin Papyrus?

The Egyptians had left hundreds of old mine workings dotted along the Wadi Hammamat, many of which had been located, and he'd heard reports that mining exploration companies had brought some of them back to life.

But he couldn't imagine Egyptologists embarking on a gold mining quest, even less, digging up gold-bearing quartzite before pounding it into powder, smelting the gold and pouring it into ingots.

An arduous process.

And an altogether long shot with no certainty of a return.

There had to be more to it.

But what?

A closer look at the faded illustration on the crumbling surface of the coffin base revealed faint glyphs he hadn't noticed before.

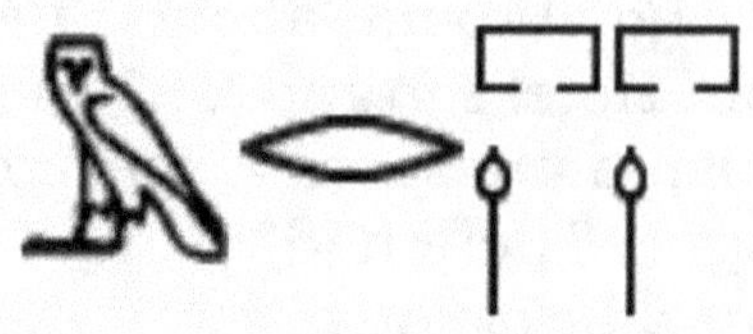

imi-r prwy hd

The text appeared like an annotation above a certain jaggedly square mountain feature shaped rather like a stepped pyramid.

He translated the text as 'Overseer of the Treasury... of Seth'

Above the oddly-shaped mountain sat a drawn symbol of the Seth animal with its peculiar split tail.

Did this message identify the tomb coffin as belonging to an important official, an Overseer of the Treasury of the god Seth?

Or did it mark the site of the Overseer's Treasury itself? The Treasury of the god Seth?

Seth marks the spot.

A treasury located in far-off Wadi Hammamat?

Why would they locate it there?

It would be nearer to the gold supply, yes, but perhaps there was another reason for stashing it in such a remote site. Security. A protection against seizure by future pharaohs and other religious institutions - a common enough practice - and looting by possible foreign conquerors such as the Assyrians, Persians or one day even the Kush of Nubia.

Maybe this was a secret record of a hidden golden cache, disguised as an underworld Book of Ways, one that only the future initiated could interpret?

The initiated, and one other person... a scholar of the Egyptian underworld, Professor David Harvardson.

Daniel glanced at his watch.

It was past midnight.

He would bring this revelation to the attention of the SCA official Ahmed Khalid first in the morning, before they set off for the next day of the congress.

What did the suspects plan to do next?

He ran into the author Jemma Karnak in the foyer, after buzzing Khalid to come downstairs for an urgent discussion.

"I've been snooping around a bit, Daniel," Jemma said, looking excited. "Somebody saw Nadine and Carlton check out of the hotel last night right after the Congress, skipping the opera. I dug around a bit more at reception. It appears they left with a pair of Egyptians in a four-wheel drive vehicle."

He nodded.

"That stacks up."

"What do you mean? You don't look at all surprised. The truth, please. I'm your partner in crime, remember."

He couldn't lie to her.

He described the apparent illustration of a Book of Two Ways that he'd spotted on the crumbling floor of a coffin and his conviction that it was something more.

"I believe it's a map of a section of the Wadi Hammamat, revealing a hidden secret. An inscription mentions the Overseer of the Treasury of the god Seth and marks a site with the symbol of the Seth animal."

"But the tomb was said to be totally free of inscriptions of any kind," Jemma protested. "And according to the published reports the coffin was found to be degraded beyond restoration - reduced to sawdust."

"Exactly what threw me."

"A map leading to a second cache of some sort?" Jemma shook her head with a look of weary resignation in her eyes. "Then I was robbed not once, but *twice*. Funny how one event can trigger another."

Khalid joined them, a hopeful look on his face. He must have picked up the note of intrigue in Daniel's voice when he'd buzzed him to come down.

Daniel briefed him urgently, adding, "We know where they're going."

"Then we go straight to Wadi Hammamat after them," Khalid said. "I'll make immediate arrangements."

"I hope you're including me," Jemma said.

"This is official business," the official said.

"But you're forgetting, I spent years with David as an archaeologist exploring that Wadi!"

"Let her come. I think it's important she be there," Daniel said.

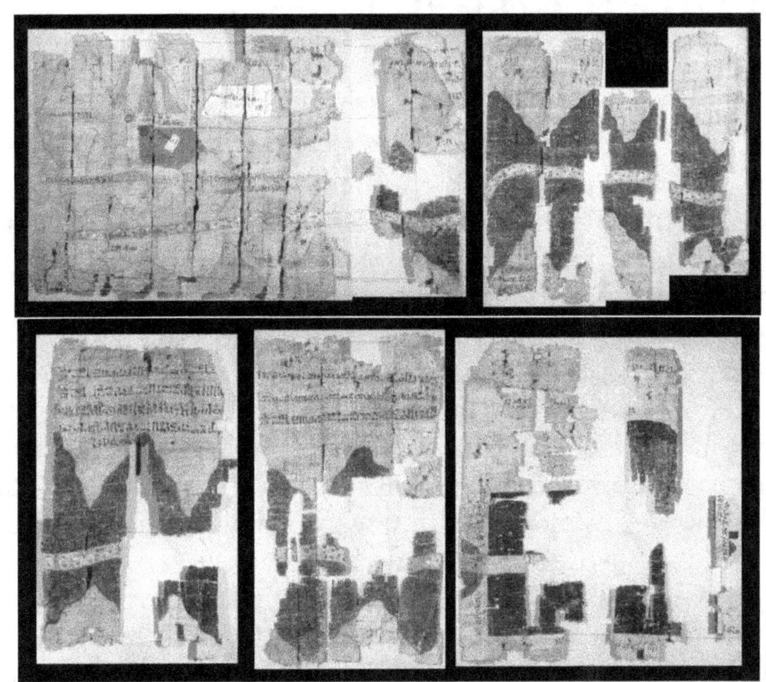

Ancient Turin Papyrus - map of Wadi Hammamat Wikipedia

CHAPTER 11
Wadi Hammamat

They hammered through the heat and rocky terrain between the Nile and the Red Sea in a pair of four-wheel drive vehicles, joined by uniformed soldiers with machine guns, and guided by an official from Aswan, the supervisor of the Ancient Mines and Quarries Department in the Ministry of Antiquities, who knew the Wadi Hammamat as well as any.

They followed not a printout from Google Earth, but a print out of a faded ancient Egyptian map at least four thousand years old and they were now bouncing around off-road across desolate shale and rock.

It was a map astonishingly ahead of its time.

It showed different coloured hills and peaks and the colours of iron oxide and the green rock of silicate, the vector that pointed to gold, even the coloured spots that indicated different gravel, recording hills and peaks of different shapes, reds, pink and green and dark basalt stone.

"We are following in the tracks of pharaonic miners," the Aswan-based Mines and Quarries Supervisor said.

"They came for gold and for precious stone. Pharaohs like Rameses and Senusert would send thousands of men to quarry their prized *Bekhen*-stone, which geologically speaking was metagraywacke sandstone and siltstone, in order to create hundreds of fine statues and sphinxes."

"It's not only a mine of precious stone and gold, this place is also a mine of inscriptions," Jemma Karnak said. "The cliffs are full of records of expeditions and references to pharaohs across the dynasties, including Narmer, the first king of all, who unified Egypt."

These sweltering valleys were a crucible of greed, Daniel thought, a melting slag of gold mines, garrisons, watchtowers, abandoned stone sarcophagi and rock inscriptions left by those who had toiled and died here. They went through a gorge between jagged mountains like black pyramids.

They spotted a flash of sun on a windscreen, a vehicle hidden at the foot a ragged, step-pyramid shaped mountain of red stone - red, the colour of the god Seth - and they stopped, out of sight, and advanced on foot.
But their quarry had set a guard on their treasure.
A shot rang out, probably meant for one of the armed guards, but it was Jemma Kanak who gave a cry and spun to the ground near a boulder.
The others took cover and a shocked Daniel dived to Jemma's side.
She had taken a bullet to the body and blood had already spread from her lips like melting lipstick.
"So I am to be denied again, at the end," she said. "I am sorry, Daniel."
"I know, Jemma. I know everything. I realized in the hotel foyer when I told you about the treasury map and you said: 'Then I was robbed not once, but *twice*.' Yes, you had been tomb-robbed by a betraying husband - robbed of a tomb discovery that should have been yours too. You flung the accusation in a written curse. Tomb Robber, may the scorpions' stings be against you and your greed, and strike with the fire of the god's anger. And you said something else in the foyer. 'Funny how one event can trigger another.' And then it hit me. You began a chain reaction by killing just one of the team. Not Harvardson, that would have been too obvious. Just another of the team members, knowing that powerful greed, fear and suspicion would compound the situation, triggering a murderous chain reaction, as you planned..."

"Author! Author, Daniel! You've mastered plot construction. And you were right, a woman did prefer using poison as a murder weapon. The venom of scorpions." She coughed.

"Don't speak any more."

"I didn't want to write any more mysteries, you see. So I decided to *live* one myself, my last murder mystery. David and I hadn't seen each other since the divorce and the Great Return to Egypt gave me the perfect opportunity. I had bided my time. But you know the serving suggestion for the dish of revenge? Best served cold."

Jemma Karnak slipped away from him before the gun battle began.

"You stay with her, while we go forward," Khadir said, advancing with the armed soldiers and the other Egyptian man behind the cover of rocks.

"It's too late," Daniel said.

He gave a last, long look at Jemma Karnak.

"You won't be ending up at the end of a *halfa* grass rope," he murmured.

He broke away and followed after the others.

It was just as well that he had lagged behind. One of the defenders had been circling them and he appeared out of a craggy outcrop, a rifle in hand, lifting it to fire at the advancing team.

Daniel spotted a curved rock at his feet shaped as if to fit into the hand and might once have been used crush quartzite ore for gold. He gripped it.

The attacker was a few metres away from him, aiming the rifle now.

Daniel spring-loaded his muscles and shot forward, holding up the gold grinding stone like a pharaoh's stone mace poised to strike.

It was the iconic smiting scene depicted on a myriad of temple scenes brought sickeningly to life.

Daniel crashed the stone on the attacker's head, smashing his skull.

The Egyptian soldiers and the Antiquities men made a charge forward.

Two defenders fell to their machine gun fire, the Egyptian pair Daniel had seen on the Hotel Terrace in a meeting with the new widow and her archaeological team member, the epigraphy expert, who had no doubt confirmed that the map on the coffin base led not through the underworld, but to a golden treasury.

Nadine and Carlton offered no resistance when they arrived.

"We found it," Nadine said, standing in front of an entrance they had blasted open. Black shadow gaped in the side of the jagged, step-pyramid mountain.

"Did you strike gold?" Daniel said.

"See for yourself."

They did, bathing the inside of a vaulted cavern in a flashlight.

Gold ingots and treasures shouted an answer.

What kind or shriveled soul did not want to find a cache of gold, Nadine had said, quoting words of a presentation Professor Harvardson had written. And here it was, the pure, imperishable 'flesh of the gods' piled in ingots and reborn in a collection of statues, masks, urns, slender necked vases, casket, shrines and jewellery. But most of all ingots, towers of ancient, solid gold bars.

It was one thing to try to dispose of golden artefacts, but this was precious, untraceable currency.

The pure ancient gold of Egypt - a temptation to kill for.

How did they ever hope to ferry the gold away?

Her epigraphic partner Carlton provided the answer.

"Mineral exploration companies still work this ancient route all the time. A heavy-lift helicopter flying in low over the desert from the Red Sea would probably not have been noticed."

"There you have it," Daniel said to the SCA official. "I doubt this drama is going to scare your international tourism away. It should end up attracting even more visitors to Egypt and to the far south."

"Egypt owes you a great debt," Khadir said.

But Daniel wondered. Did he want that debt repaid? Would this golden treasure sanctuary, hidden in the underworld like the dying sun at night, whet his appetite for more archaeology?

Or cloy it with its rich and glittering excess?

CHAPTER 12
The cycle of murder

"Jemma Karnak succeeded till the end, dreaming up a plot that baffled me. I couldn't pick the killer in her," Kate said. "It's devastating."

"I think the impact of what happened to her, how she was wronged by her former partner in marriage and in archaeology, was devastating for her too. It gave her a motive that's hard for others to grasp and that could only arise in her and in her situation. And no amount of catharsis through writing about murder was enough to heal the wound. She never entirely made the crossover from Egyptologist to detective in crime," he said, "ironic as that sounds, coming from me."

"And that single act of revenge by her against one of the team sparked the cycle of killings?" Kate said.

"It did. They'd suppressed their greed for a long time and neurotic fear and suspicion had a chance to fester. To keep their silence and complicity that long, Harvardson must have told them what the map in the coffin promised, yet only Harvardson possessed an image of the actual, detailed map. One act of violence against their number was enough to trigger a cycle."

"Do you think the Biblical archaeology sponsor may have been right? That the malevolence from the Seth tomb went on spreading a cycle of death?"

He shrugged.

"That cycle has been with us for a long time. Think of Cain's murder of his brother Abel in Genesis, and Seth's murder of his brother Osiris in ancient Egyptian mythology."

"What will happen now?"

He glanced at the little amuletic figure hanging on the chain around her neck.

Maat, goddess of justice, judgement and truth.

She would have her day now, Daniel thought.
And he thought of his own secret mark of truth.

The end

Mystery of Egypt Collection by Roy Lester Pond

The Egyptian adventure series featuring Anson Hunter, alternative Egyptologist, battling dangers from the ancient past:-

ANSON HUNTER ARCHAEOLOGY THRILLERS

The first three Anson Hunter novels in the 9-novel series – in one Kindle edition. Fiction's favourite independent, renegade Egyptologist. The Smiting Texts, Hathor's Holocaust, The Ibis Apocalypse
*****5-star fiction Amazon/Goodreads

THE EGYPTIAN MYTHOLOGY MURDERS

A mummy named Isis is taken to a hospital for a non-invasive imaging scan... so begins a mystery and a string of deaths.
An ancient cycle unfolds in modern day London - and a search for eternal love.
Can Jennefer, a young trainee museum curator and Jon, a police antiquities unit detective, stop the killings in time before a terrible culmination of events?

The EGYPTIAN OBELISK Prophecy

What was the Obelisk Prophecy?
The exciting fiction sequel to 'The Egyptian Mythology Murders'.
Detectives and Egyptologists are in sister professions.
Now the unusual team of Jennefer, an Egyptologist museum curator, and Jon, an arts and antiquities policeman, is back together in 'The Obelisk Prophecy".
Egyptian obelisks are potent symbols that pierce the skies around the world. London, New York, The Vatican...
But now one obelisk represents the clue to a world-threatening mystery.
Working against secret enemies the team must race to find and penetrate the riddle of the one obelisk on earth that holds the key to salvation.

THE EGYPTIAN CROCODILE QUEEN

When a new blockbuster ancient Egyptian exhibition arrives, mysterious events and a string of killings soon follow.
The investigative team of Jennefer, a curator, and Jon a police antiquities detective, must track down the shocking truth in a hidden underworld beneath the city - and discover a shocking secret from ancient Egypt, linked to a modern day conspiracy that takes its impetus from the ancient past.
In the unnerving footsteps of THE EGYPTIAN MYTHOLOGY MURDERS and THE OBELISK PROPHECY.

THE EGYPTIAN MUMMY WRAP MURDERS

4th book in the enthralling 'Egyptian Mythology Murders' mystery series.
The spell of a vintage reel of film shot at a dig site in Egypt in the early 1900s.
A crumbling mummy in the private museum collection of a Grand English Castle today.
A mummy called Nephthys, the same name as the Egyptian goddess who wove the cloth mummy wrappings of Osiris, called the 'Tresses of Nephthys'.
A series of graphic murders...
Is the terrifying onslaught building to an event that will affect the world?
And what is the secret of the eerie, nonverbal young daughter of the Earl?

Investigative team of Jennefer, a British Museum Egyptologist Curator, and her partner Jon, an Antiques Unit Detective, have just hours to stop a countdown to catastrophe.

TRILOGY. THE EGYPTIAN MYTHOLOGY MURDERS: 3 TITLES IN ONE EDITION

Ancient Egypt resurrected...
3 Egyptian mythology-driven mystery thrillers set in the modern day, but with a twist of the ancient unknown.
A unique investigative team of Jennefer, a museum curator, and Jon a London antiquities detective - two very different people who work in 'kindred professions'...
The X-Files meets 'The Mummy'...
- THE EGYPTIAN MYTHOLOGY MURDERS
A mummy named Isis is taken to a hospital for a non-invasive imaging scan... so begins a mystery and a string of deaths.
An ancient cycle unfolds in modern day London - and a search for eternal love.
Can Jennefer, a young trainee museum curator and

Jon, a police antiquities unit detective, stop the killings in time before a terrible culmination of events?
- OBELISK One Egyptian obelisk is the key to saving civilization
- THE CROCODILE QUEEN MYSYERY An Egypt exhibition, a series of mythological murders

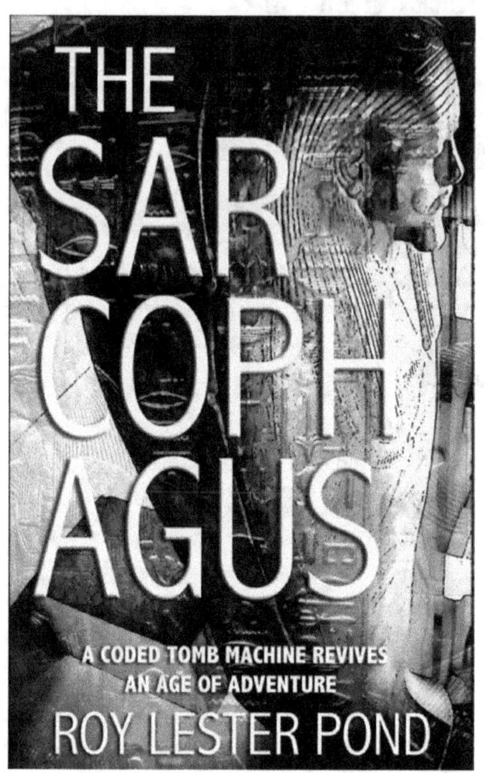

THE SARCOPHAGUS

Adventure, mystery, fantasy. An archaeologist with a
bow shoots an arrow into adventure...
In the modern age, Ryder an archaeologist in Egypt
discovers a mysterious empty sarcophagus in a tomb.
Then his Egyptologist partner Janet goes missing.
He vows to go after her, even if it means journeying
across the boundaries of reason and existence. Ahead of
Ryder and his Ridgeback dog lies a pre-dynastic realm
of myth: the mysterious Mistress of the Bow and Ruler
of Arrows, the evil Lord Set, legions of animal-headed
creatures, the venerable bird-man, the child Horus. And
key to it all is the quest for the magical amulets of
power. A life-and-death struggle is on at the edge of
time. And the universe watches - and waits.

DYNASTY Zero
A primordial clash of humans, gods and demon
demigods.

A young demigod boy Nemes, a future unifier of
pharaonic Egypt, also known to history as Narmer, lived
on the fault line between deity and humanity. It was a
time of the gods and demigods, when the throne of the
god Horus shook and the weak hands of men stretched
out to catch the crown and seize the scepter of Egypt.
The demon demigods did not stand by, but seized the
moment to strike.

I, THE MUMMY
Preserved in the 'Tresses of Nephthys' - the sacred
wrappings of linen woven by the goddess Nephthys and
tied with the'magic of knotted cords' of Isis, an immortal
soldier hero rises to fight Egypt's greatest enemy - the
ruthless Hyksos invaders and occupiers...
Action adventure thriller.
Awakened after a thousand years in a tomb sanctuary
filled with weapons...
The Ancient Defender arises to fight against a ruthless
oppressor.
The Hyksos have seized Egypt at a time of weakness
following the Middle Kingdom, overpowering all with
their superior technology of chariots, hardened bronze
weapons and compound bows.
And they are now plundering Egypt for its forbidden

secrets of power.
Can ancient history's most unlikely hero stop them and
resurrect a divided land before the Hyksos can gain
Egypt's most powerful and dangerous secret of all?

THE RA JUDGEMENT
Is a vanished archaeology team member trapped in
Egypt's ancient past during an age of terror – and
sending warning messages to today?
'WARNING! ANCIENT GLOBAL THREAT…' the graffiti
message appears in a newly found Egyptian tomb, along
with a modern biohazard symbol.
What mysterious plague has hit the population of Egypt
in the reign of Pharaoh Amenhotep III and his young co-
regent, the sun-struck Akhenaten? Why is it seen as a
judgement by the angry sun god Ra? An eleventh plague
of Egypt?
Lucas, a physician and World Health Organisation
expert on pandemics, must find its source and the
antidote in time to save the ancient past and the future.

Especially when his lover, Egyptologist Giulietta in the modern age, is exposed to the deadly contagion. Can he warn her in time and save her - and can they ever hope to be reunited?

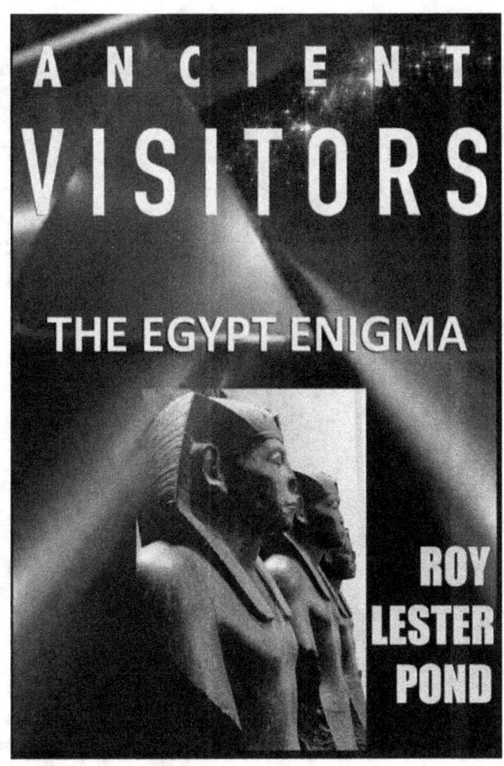

'Ancient VISITORS The Egypt Enigma'

In the field of ancient civilizations, 'visitors' meant one thing to Egyptologist Rebecca Landers.
The controversial theory about the enigma of Egypt and its advanced technological achievements.
Then came the surprising evidence... and a threat to the world.
Suddenly she and her team were called on to span two worlds on a dangerous archaeological quest like no other.
Only they had the power to save history and the future.

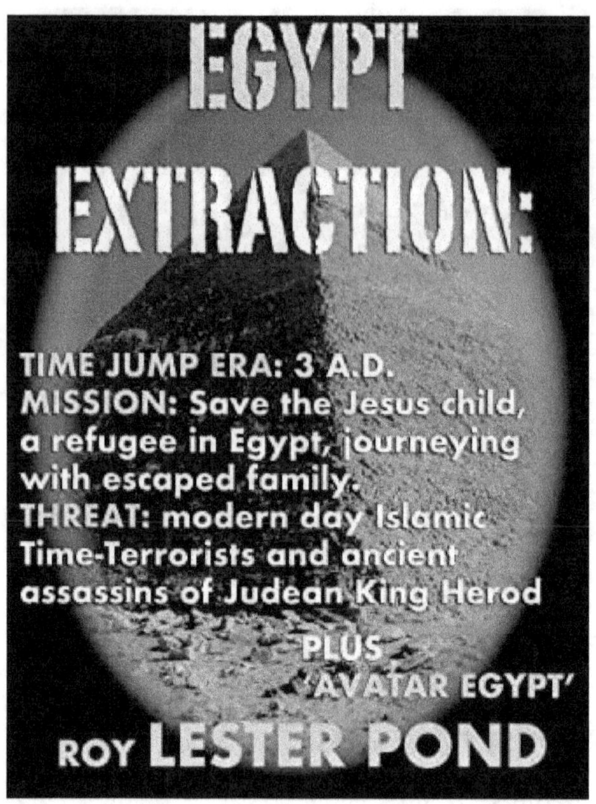

EGYPT EXTRACTION
TIME JUMP ERA: 3 A.D.
MISSION: Save the Jesus child, a refugee in Egypt, journeying with escaped family.
THREAT: modern day Islamic Time-Terrorists and ancient assassins of Judean King Herod...
Time-travel terrorists... drones... attackers with assault weapons racing through the Nile's papyrus reeds... their target a boy king.
At stake, the future of civilization.
Standing in their way, two young time jumpers, Salome and Callen of the Anti Time-Terrorist Strike Force. They must stop a catastrophe that could affect billions of lives and the belief systems of the world. Sci-fi, ancient history and time-travel novella with a startling twist and revelation.

Plus AVATAR EGYPT
An ancient Egyptian simulator game turns deadly real.

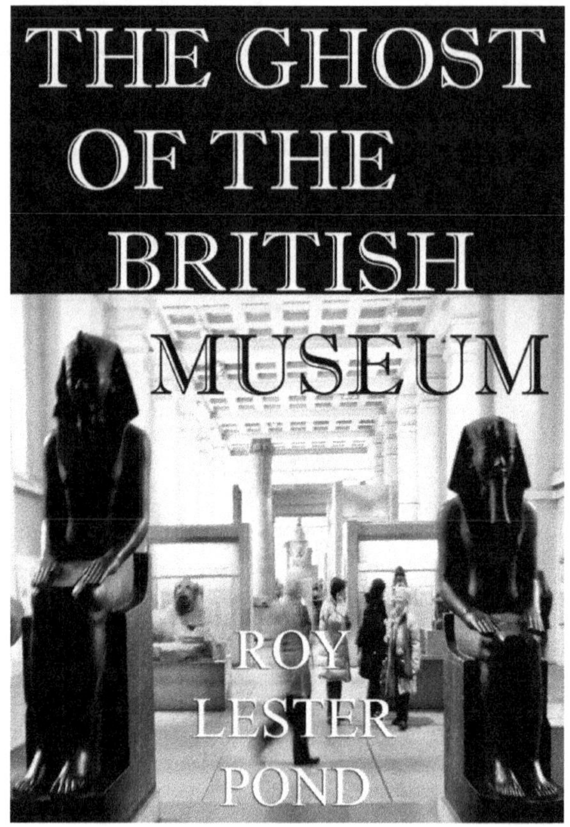

THE GHOST OF THE BRITISH MUSEUM

There is a certain statue in the Sculpture Gallery of the
British Museum of the son of Rameses The Great,
Egypt's most illustrious pharaoh.
The statue has an eerie attraction even today.
In the 1900s a London group known as The Society of
Inner Light regularly conferred with the exhibit in the
Egyptian Sculpture Gallery, convinced that it was a
medium for metaphysical activity and emanated unseen
forces.
She was an American historical writer visiting the
British Museum's Egyptian Sculpture Gallery to
research a new book.
He was a legendary and enigmatic prince from ancient

Egypt who desperately needed to undo a terrible
mistake.
Was the strange young man's sudden materialization
before Madeline just 'cosplay', or the result of an
attraction between two souls across time?
Would they share a mysterious quest on a journey
through Egypt, and much more?

EGYPT TRAP

Keep an eye on a mysteriously obsessed young wife visiting the archaeology sites of Egypt? How hard could that be?

A damaged ex-detective is hired to shadow a girl with painted eyes on a trip to Egypt...

Is she leading him step by step into a murder conspiracy and the mystery of a lost ancient Egyptian queen?

Dan Loader reluctantly accepts the job. A damaged, former-detective from a police Art and Antiques unit, he is already traumatised by an ordeal at the hands of antiquity traffickers. Yet he desperately needs something to help him hold his life together and

following the girl looks like a soft surveillance task, more so as he becomes increasingly drawn to her.
Rich, independent Kate Barnsdale is a beautiful, haunting young woman surrounded by an unmistakeable aura of ancient Egypt. Her obsession with a lost, mythic Queen from Egypt's 6th Dynasty seems to be taking over her life.
When she insists on travelling to Egypt alone to follow her mysterious urgings, her husband hires Dan to shadow her secretly and watch over her.
But is Dan being drawn step by step into a murder conspiracy that involves the secret of a mythic queen from Egypt's ancient past?
Crime and suspense with the mystery twist of ancient Egypt.

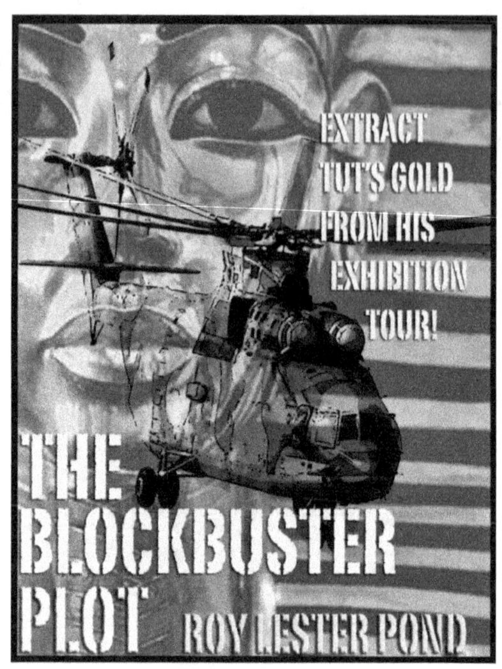

THE BLOCKBUSTER PLOT

The Boy King's Gold... a Blockbuster USA Tour... a dazzling display of criminal daring.

It was an outrageous plot:- Extract Tutankhamun's priceless gold on its blockbuster tour of the USA. *But who is the enigmatic mastermind behind the disappearing act and why have they done it?*

Will they demand a pharaoh's ransom for its return? And what will become of a pair of US hostages, a museum Egyptologist and a female National Geographic feature writer traveling with the treasures?

A golden target, the most famous treasures in the world... *gone...* the fabulous golden artefacts of Tutankhamun, about to appear in the USA in the biggest blockbuster exhibition since the world wide pandemic, have been stolen.

ONE DAY I'LL TELL YOU SOMETHING

A child obsessed with the ancient past, a young mother who discovers adventure..."

I remember Egypt," Cooper said gravely. "Long, long ago."

Her little boy was gorgeous, she thought, but his imagined past life could be a bit hard to take. Especially at 8.30 in the morning, when she was busy having a this-life crisis, running late for work and her eight-year old was about to miss his school bus.Then young single-mother Catherine meets a past life researcher and also a mysterious Egyptologist Simon Priestly and she and Cooper are off to Egypt on an extraordinary quest to follow a young boy's dreams... or are they actual memories of the ancient past?

What will they find and what will Catherine find as she

warms to the impressive British Egyptologist as they uncover a shattering secret from Egypt's past? Disturbing and intriguing adventure fiction with a twist of the unknown.

VIRTUAL EGYPT

Sci-Fi Ancient Egypt Action and Mystery in 2 novels
VIRTUAL EGYPT Running a gauntlet of gods and
guardians

Novel 1
THE EGYPT DIMENSION Ancient-Egypt inspired sci-fi
adventure fiction.

A lost pyramid structure abandoned in space...
In the future, a space archaeologist Lewis Trader and
his female archaeological android ARCHAELA make a
discovery.
A glowing ancient Egyptian-style pyramid floating
among the stars.
They begin a climb up guarded ramps inside the
structure amid rising levels of tension – their progress
challenged by mysterious, lethal guardians... leading to

a startling revelation.

Novel 2
THE VIRTUAL EGYPT GAME - a group plays a deadly
virtual reality running game inside a mysterious
simulator of ancient Egypt's dangerous underworld.
Then they start dying, for real.

THE PRINCESS WHO LOST HER SCROLL OF THE
DEAD

2 Egypt Fantasy Titles in One.
1. The Princess Who Lost Her Scroll of the Dead
Her priceless Book of the Dead is swapped for a blank
one by a greedy royal scribe... How can Nefera find her
way through the dangerous gateways and guardians of
the Egyptian underworld without her magical spells -
her passport to the world beyond?
And who is the boy tomb robber Ipy, sharing her
journey? Is he alive, or dead?

2.
MUSEUM GHOSTS
Karoy and his companions - a squad of Egyptian
wooden soldiers created to protect a tomb owner - arise

when the Lady Tiy is stolen from the museum. Can they
rescue her from the outside world?